The Silent Protocol

Another high-stakes cyber-thriller in
The Last Message Trilogy (Volume 2)

Stephen Bentley

Hendry Publishing

CONTENTS

Chapter One:
Echoes of the Past

THE LAPTOP SCREEN CASTS a pale glow on Maya's face, like a ghost that's been haunting her too long. The flat is chaos. Newspaper clippings, research notes, and coffee cups form a cluttered shrine to her obsession. In the corner, a police scanner mutters to itself, unheard. Maya sits cross-legged on a wobbly chair, exhaustion pulling at her limbs. Hair unwashed, eyes ringed with shadows. Fingers flying across the keys, she is ferocious. Determined. A cipher of unreadable text appears on her monitor, blinking like a taunt, and Maya smiles through her fatigue. She's close. Outside, London flickers with police sirens and occasional blackouts, a city still reeling twelve years after the VEGA incident. But Maya barely notices, her focus a tightrope stretched thin. She chews on a thumbnail, launches her decryption software, and waits. The lines of code tremble, transform. Her eyes widen at the words forming on the screen. "Protocol Silence." "Coordinated communications blackout." Her heart jumps to match the speed of her typing.

Stacks of notes threaten to topple. The clatter of a coffee cup echoes as it hits the floor. Maya doesn't flinch. A laptop bag sits discarded in the corner, half-buried under layers of newspapers. Clippings hang from the walls like a serial killer's map, connected by strings of highlighted text and black ink circles. Government corruption. Surveillance scandals. Phrases like "Unresolved" and "Ongoing Investigation" scream from every headline. The window rattles with the hum of sirens, distant but persistent. This city has been sick for twelve years, she thinks. All of it starting with the VEGA incident, and the virus that spread faster than the authorities' lies. They'd promised a return to normal. What a joke.

Her hands move over the keys with the precision of a surgeon, pulse quickening with every tap. She pushes her hair out of her eyes, the strands refusing to cooperate. Tired, yes, but sharper than ever. The past weeks a blur of late nights and takeout dinners, cold when she remembers to eat them. Not enough hours. Never enough. The newest file looks promising. Her eyes flicker from screen to paper, notes filled with hastily scribbled names and dates. A timeline of deceit.

Maya stretches her neck and winces. The muscles protest. A sharp ache at the base of her skull, dull but constant. She ignores it. The corner of her laptop shows the time—nearly two A.M. Someone across town screams; someone else is smashing bottles. Life in the cracks of a broken promise. She knows she should sleep, knows her body is ready to collapse, but she leans forward, more determined than ever.

A stray takeout container teeters on the edge of the desk. Aged soy sauce crusts its rim. She shoves it aside, makes space for her cup of stone-cold coffee. Takes a swig. Bitter, like it should be. A text message buzzes on her phone—three words from her editor: Anything on Parallax? She tosses the phone back into the clutter. Silence her only answer. If he only knew.

Her attention darts back to the laptop, to the file that refuses to let go of her. Unreadable characters fill the screen. Maya smirks at them, a challenge more than an obstacle. She stretches her fingers, the joints stiff, and types with new urgency. Through her contacts, she's acquired software so specialized she sometimes wonders if she's on a watchlist. Screw them, she thinks. Let them watch. She launches the decryption program, checks her notes, and feels the anticipation like caffeine injected straight into her veins.

The police scanner rattles off an unintelligible stream, white noise against the stillness. It joins the scattered soundtrack of Maya's life: clicking keys, growling stomach, laptop fan working overtime. She tunes it all out. Focus, she reminds herself. Focus or die. The file name taunts her with its vagueness. Discreet. Anonymous. The kind that can get a person killed. She can't wait to see what it hides.

Newspaper clippings form a border around the walls. Her life inside those margins, it sometimes seems. Maya rolls her neck again, listens to it pop, wills herself to stay awake. To stay sharp. Takeout boxes pile up in a trash bin by the desk. Thai. Indian. Something else she doesn't even remember ordering. At least three different meals, half-finished. Beside them, old photographs, blurred from age and too many thumbtacks. Faces from the past that should be helping her. Faces she's learned she can't trust.

The decryption program chews on the file, blue bars pulsing like a heartbeat. Maya stares at it, unblinking. Impatience crawls up her spine. She knows it takes time. Knows the intricacies. But every second drags, taut like a tripwire. She rubs her eyes and waits. The software whirs, strings of code vibrating with potential. Soon. Soon.

A low rumble from the window. London in chaos, as usual. The street below bathed in the yellow glow of generators. Stuttering light across bricks and faces. Maya ignores it, her world confined to the four corners of her screen. Her breathing grows shallow, anticipation edging out fatigue. This is it. She feels it in her bones. This is it.

Lines shift on the monitor, code dissolving to legibility. Words emerge from the digital fog. "Protocol Silence." "Communications blackout." Her heart jumps. Fingers frozen over the keyboard. This is it, she thinks. This is really it. A trail she hadn't even known she was chasing. Her eyes widen, disbelief giving way to exhilaration. She bites her lip and digs deeper, capturing everything. Documenting. Bracing herself against the magnitude of what she's found.

Panic and elation twist through her chest. Thoughts racing. What the hell is Protocol Silence? She can almost feel the tremor of urgency in the air, electric and charged. If she wasn't awake before, she sure as hell is now. She scans the lines again, searching for more, the reality of the discovery pounding through her with every rapid breath.

The room around her closes in, each item a reminder of how deep she's gone. How deep she still needs to go. She pushes hair back from her face and focuses, driven by the promise of what these fragments might mean. Hands steady despite the adrenaline, Maya works through the night, pulling on threads she didn't know she held, following a conspiracy she's only begun to unravel.

A stray sunbeam slashes across the laptop screen, obliterating the letters like a government censor. Maya tilts the monitor away from the window, checks her phone again, keeps pacing. No missed calls, no texts. What the hell, Bhatti? The file waits, open and unreadable from this distance, a threat lurking in plain sight. The final stretch of exhaustion pulls at her bones. Pulls at her nerves. If she can just talk to him, make him see how big this is. If she can make anyone see. A voice finally crackles on the line. Bhatti. Cautious, like he's already playing for both sides. "It's been a while, Maya." She grips the phone tighter, plants her elbow on the stack of papers that serves as a countertop. "I found something. Protocol Silence. It's big." A pause stretches across the ocean of static. Her foot taps against the linoleum in furious impatience. His answer is a million miles away.

"Maya. Slow down." His voice, straining for control. It pushes against her urgency like a kid holding back a flood. She breathes out a sigh that's more frustration than air. Eyes locked on the laptop, on the words that could set this whole city ablaze. "It mentions a communications blackout." A slight tremor in her voice now, or maybe it's the phone line, more crowded than a conference call. "Bhatti. Did you hear me?"

The line crackles. "I heard." Detached. Almost tired. "Twelve years, and you still can't let it go."

Twelve years, she thinks, and Bhatti is still a detective sergeant. The rest of the world already has let it go. She knows him too well. Knows he won't take this seriously until he's staring it in the face. Knows he won't trust her until it's too late. Her hand drums against the cabinet door. Open. Shut. Open.

"This is something else," she says. "Not Parallax. It's all here. Satellite networks. System vulnerabilities. They're planning another attack, Bhatti." A thrill of terror shoots through her. A thrill of excitement too. She needs him to say something. Anything. Needs him to stop acting like this is a social call.

She can hear him breathe. A world of empty space on the line, in the air, between them. "Meet me at the usual place. One hour." He's all cop now, short on time and shorter on promises.

"Not over the phone." She doesn't know why she says it; they've never been on the same side of a conversation, much less a war. "I can't trust anyone with this. Not even you."

"Meet me," he repeats. "And be careful, Maya. You're not the only one still listening."

The line clicks, once, twice. Hangs dead like a man on the gallows. Maya stares at the phone, the walls, the city beyond. All of it closing in. The corners of the room tightening like a noose. She throws the phone onto the table and rushes to the laptop. It's still there, still menacing. The file taunts her in plain sight. She copies it to another drive, two drives, three. Labelling each with a hand too rushed to read later. She can't risk leaving them all here. Can't risk taking them all with her. The radio static from the scanner cuts in and out, background noise to a threat she still can't believe. Not all of it, anyway.

She jams the drives under couch cushions, under piles of takeout boxes, under the loose tile near the door. They can tear this place apart, she thinks. They can tear it all apart, but they won't find me. She knows how to run. Learned from the best. A dull ache shoots through her chest, like guilt wrapped in barbed wire. Or maybe it's just too many late nights and cigarettes.

Outside, the sound of sirens, louder now. Closer. She checks the locks on the windows, the locks on the door. Wonders how long she's been here, this time. Wonders how long they've been watching. They? Don't be stupid. Don't get paranoid. Keep moving, Maya. Keep moving or you're already dead.

The minutes stretch like a bad cartoon, figures elongated and ridiculous. She imagines them kicking down the door, faces she almost trusts. Almost. She copies the file again, losing track of how many versions she's made. Paranoia runs through her veins like quicksilver. Or the truth. She doesn't know the difference anymore.

She tears her jacket from the back of a chair, throws the hood over her head. She can do this. She has to do this. Footsteps echo up the stairs, and she holds her breath until they pass. The edges of the room bend and shift. She's a refugee from her own story. A refugee with enough evidence to start another.

Maya slips the last drive into her boot, wincing at the hard edges. It digs into her skin like a promise. Be careful, he said. She almost laughs. There's never been room for careful. Not then. Not now. She's out the door and into the stairwell before she remembers her keys.

Chapter Two:
Shadows and Warnings

The light flickers and Maya jumps. She checks her phone again, every buzz of the sticky pub's neon sign raising her heart rate by a few dozen beats. DS Bhatti appears in the doorway like an exhausted ghost, his shoulders hunched against the evening cold. His face is a map of things she doesn't want to know, and the tight set of his mouth means trouble. His eyes skim the nearly empty room before he makes his way toward her, trench coat and concern billowing around him like they're part of the same lousy deal.

Bhatti slides into the seat without removing his coat. The sticky floor moans beneath him. He pauses before speaking, lets his eyes roam the flickering lights.

"Are we being watched?" Maya can't hide the urgency. She keeps her voice low, an instinct born of too much time doing things she shouldn't.

"Are you expecting anyone?" He answers with a question, and Maya shifts, uncomfortable.

"I was expecting you ten minutes ago."

"Good. That means I'm unpredictable."

"Don't do this to me." Her voice almost cracks. "What's going on?"

A trace of something close to sympathy moves across his face, quick as a blink. "Is your drink even touched?"

"Is that what we're worried about?"

Bhatti doesn't reply. He leans back, makes a show of letting his eyes wander over the peeling wallpaper, the smeared windows. Two men drink silently at the bar, both lost in their own private worlds of alcohol and regret.

He nods toward her glass. "Drink it or don't, but don't let them see you watching it."

She almost laughs. "I thought that was our thing. Watching things."

He almost smiles, but his eyes don't follow suit. They still look tired and nervous. "You've been watching the door more than the drink."

"That means I'm predictable." The flickering lights cast the room in seizure-inducing shadows. She tries again, tries to get a straight answer. "What's with the look?"

"It's my face."

"Very funny. It's not your face. It's the other thing. The slumped-shoulder, wild-eyed, ready-to-piss-your-self thing."

"That's my look."

"It's not your look. It's your 'something very bad is happening' look."

Bhatti hesitates, and in that pause Maya's stomach drops. His concern suddenly feels like a weight, like an accusation. She sees the message before it leaves his mouth.

He leans forward, keeping his voice low. "Someone's put a kill order on your head."

Her hand freezes mid-air. She can't bring it down, can't reach her drink or reach anything. The room spins around her, sticky floors and stale beer tilting together until they stop making sense.

Bhatti doesn't say anything. He waits, watching as the colour leaves her face.

"How—how do you know?" The words come out slow and dull, like her brain's gone numb.

"You have your networks, I have mine."

"And you know who? Why? This is a scare tactic."

"You've scared someone, that's certain."

"Then I'll lie low, change—"

Bhatti shakes his head, cutting her off. "No change of address will fix this one, Maya."

"So it's serious?" She's breathing hard now. Her voice carries a hint of hope that she knows she shouldn't hold on to.

"No one's laughing."

Her breath steadies, the anger creeping back in. "But why? They can't be this scared. I'm not even that close."

"It doesn't matter how close you think you are. It matters how close they think you are."

"And what? I just stop?"

"You disappear."

"This investigation, it's—" she starts.

"Don't say too much."

Maya catches herself, takes a deep breath. Bhatti's warning sinks in deeper than any pool deep end. Her pulse is in her ears, her chest, her fingers. "This is big, Bhatti. If I quit now—"

"None of it matters if you're dead."

She tries to hold his gaze, tries to argue with it, but his eyes don't blink, and she's forced to look away.

He pushes his chair back, keeps his voice as steady as he can. "Your life is important to you?"

"It's not my first priority."

"Maybe it should be."

"It never was yours."

"That's why I'm still alive."

They sit in silence for a moment, the hollow void pressing down until Maya can hardly breathe. The pub is still mostly empty, but it feels full now, too full, like the two men at the bar and the two flickering lights have multiplied and surrounded them with strangers.

Bhatti stands to leave. His eyes say more than his voice ever could. She hates him for that, hates him for being right, for scaring her, for saving her life.

"I'll take precautions," she finally says. The resignation in her voice tastes like blood in her mouth. "But I'm not quitting."

"You're as stubborn as I thought."

She forces a smile. It doesn't reach her eyes. "Thanks for coming."

"If I didn't think you'd hate me more, I wouldn't have."

He reaches into his coat, pulls out a phone and hands it to her. "If things go south, call this number. No one else."

She takes it, and her hand brushes his, and for a moment she almost feels safe. Then he's gone, and all she's left with is an empty seat and a plastic burner phone that looks as cold as she feels.

Maya watches the door close behind him, and she jumps again when it slams too hard, too loud.

IN THE MIDDLE OF the night, the mountains swallow the village whole. Morning makes it new again, spitting it back out with a dusting of frost and the quiet of a held breath. Alex nods to the milkman before retreating inside, shaking off the cold like a bad memory. The small cottage has room for exactly one person, which is good, because that's all Alex can handle being. There's an inevitability to the quiet that puts him at ease. Outside, the Englishman's garden waits patiently for his attention. He makes breakfast instead. Eggs, bacon, toast, his routine as carefully constructed as his identity.

The narrow street leads through a jumble of stone houses. None of them look more than a breath away from collapsing, but Alex knows better. They've been here for centuries. They'll last longer than he will, longer than anyone with a history they're trying to escape. He moves with care, like his every step might wake the mountains.

When the neighbours see him, they smile. He nods back. They know him only as Stuart, the quiet Englishman. In the Pyrenean village, he's a part of the scenery, a natural feature of the landscape. It suits him. He prefers the anonymity. Prefers the solitude.

He comes back inside, leaves the garden for later. His phone buzzes, loud against the morning silence. Alex stops. Listens. Waits. It buzzes again. His jaw sets. He pulls the phone from his pocket, almost afraid of what it will show. The message is short. A fist to the gut.

Protocol activated. Berlin. 48 hours.

The phone shakes in his hand. He tenses, jaw clenched so tight he can feel the ache of it in his bones. He looks around the cottage like it's a stranger, like he's never seen it before.

The words blur on the screen. He blinks them back into focus, hoping they'll be different. They're not.

Protocol. Berlin. 48 hours.

He's moving before his brain catches up with his feet. Moving because there's nothing else he knows how to do. The pacing helps, but only a little. He holds the phone in one hand, a lifeline or a death sentence or both. He starts tracing the message, breaking it down and retracing. When he's done, his lips are drawn in a tight line. Whoever sent it is clever. A ghost.

Alex breathes out, steady as he can. It's been too long. He thought he'd cut all ties. But here it is. A simple text, complicated as hell. He keeps moving, each lap of the cottage forcing his brain into action.

They can't reach him here.

They already have.

Maybe it's a mistake.

Maybe it's a trap.

The small stone house seems smaller with every step. It closes in on him, air thick with frost and fear and a desperation he hasn't felt in years. He stops pacing, thinks, lets his brain calculate the risk. A series of pros and cons, variables and unknowns. Every outcome is the same.

"Damn it all to hell."

His words are a death knell to the life he's built. A start. An end. The inevitability of it crashes over him, but this time he's ready for the wave. He destroys the phone, careful, quick. There's nothing left of it when he's done. Just shards. Just plastic.

The chest under the bed hasn't been opened since he got here. Not once. The lock takes him longer than it should. Not because he's forgotten the combination, but because turning the numbers feels like losing.

He pulls out what he needs. False passports. Cash. Documents. It's a miserable feeling, having your life reduced to things you can fit in a bag. He's been here before.

An old habit makes him go to the window, makes him check the escape routes. Two roads lead out of the village. The locals never bother with the second one. Alex will. He knows it's easier. He's planned for this. A worst-case scenario. A worst-case life.

The documents go in first. Clothes, barely enough to last a week. He moves like a ghost, leaving nothing but shadows and memories. Memories the neighbours will dismiss. They never really knew him anyway.

His breath makes small clouds in the cold morning air. It feels heavier outside. Unforgiving. He tightens the bag over his shoulder, knots it like a noose. He stands at the door longer than he should. There's nothing left to wait for, but he waits anyway.

Alex disappears like he's done it before. And he has. He disappears the way the night disappears. He disappears like a pro.

The small cottage is empty again. The mountains reclaim the village. The garden waits. The chest stays locked under the bed.

Chapter Three: Uneasy Reunion

CIGARETTE BUTTS DECORATE THE pavement, drowning in puddles of rainwater and old chewing gum. The drizzle has soaked everything, leaving the streets gleaming with a slick shine that turns them into rivers of blurred neon and shadows. He waits in the darkness, shoulders hunched, a phantom with eyes fixed on the lit window above. Curtains move, then settle, and the outline of her body shifts behind glass, pacing. He lights another cigarette, its flare a tiny explosion in the wet night. When he moves, it's mainly with certainty but also a shiver of doubt, crossing the street and its reflections in long strides. By the time he reaches the door, his hair is plastered to his head, and he shakes it off like a dog, a wry smile playing on his lips as he raps his knuckles against wood.

The shadow hesitates at the entrance, letting his eyes and ears work. The hum of an upstairs television, the distant sirens, a door slamming two floors above. He looks for cameras, escape routes, anything out of place. The same old habits. Paranoia. The rain picks up, so he tries the doorbell. The sound of footsteps, then silence. His fingers twitch with impatience. She's in there, definitely.

A narrow hallway leads to the staircase. A glassy-eyed dog sleeps in the foyer, oblivious to the door creaking open. When he's halfway up, she's already waiting at the top of the stairs, holding a taser. Eyes bright and wide. He moves slowly, hands out in surrender.

"You've got to be fucking kidding me," Maya says, lowering the weapon. Her mouth hangs open, a mix of disbelief and something else, some deeper frustration. She steps aside to let him in, careful to keep her distance. He knows this move. Defence and suspicion. He knows her well.

"Maya," he says. The name feels odd on his tongue after all these years. He doesn't make a move to hug her, doesn't even offer a handshake.

He's older, sure, but it's definitely him. Thin, sharp like a knife, with more silver flecks in his hair than she remembers.

"You haven't changed," he says.

"Where the hell have you been?" she asks, closing the door behind them.

The room is a frenzy. Wall-to-wall with chaos. Laptops on every surface, code flickering, wires snaking across the floor like some technical pit of vipers. Clippings and notes plaster every wall. Empty coffee cups pile up, spilling over onto the crowded table and window ledges. She's got a hell of a setup, impressive and suffocating.

Alex shrugs off his damp coat. The suit underneath is crisp, anachronistic. "You've been busy." His eyes sweep the room, then land back on her.

"You shouldn't have come here." Her words are a wall. "You don't get to show up after all this time. No warning."

He opens his mouth, pauses. The look on his face is of someone trying to solve a puzzle. "Yes. Well."

"What do you want?" Maya's arms cross, the taser still in one hand. She doesn't ask him to sit. Doesn't ask if he wants coffee. She paces in front of the biggest monitor, footsteps finding spaces on the cluttered floor.

He takes out a phone. Not hers; his. A battered old burner. He shows her the screen, two words that suck the anger out of the room and leave it hollow. "Protocol Silence," he says.

Maya's face changes. All heat, no light. A ghost passes between them, this thing they thought was dead. "You got this?" Her voice lowers. Almost a whisper.

"This morning." He puts the phone back in his pocket, his movements measured. "It seems I am still worth finding."

She doesn't like the sound of that. She's suddenly all motion, sweeping cups and papers to one side of the table to clear a space. "This is bigger than you, Alex. Bigger than both of us."

He watches as she digs into the digital mountain in front of her, pulling out a hard drive and hooking it to the nearest laptop. Clippings drift to the floor. Her fingers fly over keys. She's not the only one who can disappear into her work.

"The fragment I decrypted yesterday." Maya stops, looks at him, an intensity that's new. "It's a shutdown. Massive. These arseholes are planning something big."

He sits finally, leaning forward, elbows on knees. "Who?"

She glances back at the wall, then the screen. An infinite spiderweb of connections. "The same players," she says.

"And some new ones." Her breath is quick, her words quicker. "Satellite deals, bribes, blackmail—"

"Then we need to move." He stands as abruptly as he sat, pacing the tiny room. His limp is pronounced when he turns, heading back her way. "I have seen this pattern before. There is no time."

"Years without a word," she says, and the accusation holds more hurt than she intends. She looks down, busying herself with papers, anger and worry warring on her face. "Now you show up at my door?"

"Better late than never." He's scanning again, taking mental pictures. "We can fix this, but not here. Not from this flat."

"Fix this?" She gives a sharp laugh. "You have no idea, Alex, or do you go by another name these days?"

"Stuart."

"Fucking Stuart! You are definitely not a Stuart."

She watches him check his watch. He does it twice, like the old thing is broken. She's quiet for a long minute, and in that minute, she makes a choice.

"I'm coming with you," she says. More a challenge than an offer.

He holds her gaze, unblinking. "We cannot do this like last time. We must—"

"Fuck you," she cuts him off. "Fuck Protocol Silence. Fuck running."

He looks at her, really looks. Years apart, and now here they are. Too close. Not close enough. It makes her laugh, the absurdity. The damn hopelessness of it. He hasn't changed. She still loves him. She still hates him.

Her breath catches as she closes the distance, and then they're not talking. His hand in her hair, her back against the wall, the space between them nothing now. He stops, pulls away, not letting her get too close even with his mouth against hers.

"Work first," he says, his voice more intent than before.

Maya shakes her head, wild and frantic. "Let's fuck first, then work." Her urgency matches his, and he's not arguing this time.

They stumble to the bedroom, leaving the mess, the chaos, the empty cups, the flickering screens. They leave Protocol Silence. They leave it all for now.

SHE STANDS IN THE doorframe, watching him sleep. The sheets twist around his legs like vines. Her eyes trace his form, noting the quiet rise and fall of his chest, the way his fingers curl. Like she's marking a map. For a moment, she lets herself believe this is real, this is possible, then the fear settles back in, wrapping itself around her ribcage. When he wakes, he reaches out, the world tilts, and they crash into each other. It is desperate and messy and perfect. His body against hers, heat and skin, whispering her name as if it's a secret. He tastes like cigarettes and the dark and she thinks she might love him or hate him or both. She loses herself, willingly. The second time, it's softer. He pulls her close, holds her as if to stop her from disappearing. As if he knows she might.

When they leave the bedroom, the chaos greets them like an old friend. Alex looks different, even with his shirt untucked and a day's growth on his face. Like he's come alive again, but only for a moment. He hands Maya a coffee, his touch deliberate, and they sit. Opposite ends of the table. Between them, papers, laptops, too many memories. He looks at her, really looks.

"You promised this wouldn't happen," he says. It sounds almost like a question.

"You promised a lot of things," she fires back.

It's easier to face each other across the tangle of technology, the maze of evidence. She sips her coffee, strong and bitter, before diving into the screens.

"This was you?" He nods at a laptop. A silent reference to last night's decoding.

"They'll know I accessed the files, but I'm always two steps ahead. So far." She pushes a drive across to him. "Start with that."

Alex plugs it in, fingers steady but quick. "Tell me what you have."

Her words rush out, falling over each other. "Years of digging. Silence from you, so I did my own work. Found leads. Thought I lost them. Then last month, a trace. I followed it, and everything came back."

She can see the change in his eyes, the way he dives deep into data and doesn't come up for air. "What did you think it was?"

"Wasn't sure. Then I got the message." Maya pauses, looks directly at him. "Lionel Gage?"

She doesn't miss the way he flinches, barely perceptible. The name hits them both, hard. A ghost. A threat.

He exhales, a sound that's almost a laugh. "I had hoped..." but he doesn't finish the sentence. "Someone sent it. They wanted us out of hiding."

She stands, frustrated, then sits again. "Berlin," she says.

"Too soon," he replies, the hint of a smile. It drops as he grows serious. "He won't be there. But we will learn more."

She rubs her temple, feeling the pressure of it all. Of everything. "Do you want to catch him, Alex? Or are you hoping he'll catch you?"

He holds her gaze, doesn't flinch this time. "The thought has crossed my mind." There's a familiar intensity, a recklessness she recognises.

"It's not enough just to survive this." Maya gets up, and he lets her. He knows she needs to move, needs to let her body work with her mind. She's kinetic, covering the small flat like it's the world, and he's the only one standing in it. "We take him down or we're dead anyway."

Alex runs a hand through his hair, stares at the mess in front of him. "Berlin," he agrees. He doesn't say, *We cannot do it your way*. He doesn't say, *This will kill us*.

When she sits again, it's close, and he lets her do that too. Her eyes hold his. Steady. Then they move back to the table, and everything spreads out, everything goes wide. There's an unexpected, renewed excitement in him. "This could work," he says.

Maya feels a thrill at his thrill. She catches it, sends it back his way. "I've got data on—" but he cuts her off, not wanting words, just the pure hit of collaboration.

"Yes. I see it. Right there." His voice trips and she laughs. Like a map. Like a net. Her fingers pull files off the drive as his follow right behind.

"It's bigger than VEGA," she says, daring him to follow the implications. He takes the dare. Shows her the same things from his own perspective.

"Satellite," he starts, but she already knows what he's about to say.

"Acquisitions. Communications. They have too much to hide. We have too much not to know."

She presses in. Feeds off his certainty. "This is our only lead."

He nods. The same gravity she remembers pulling them both back in. A lifetime ago. Last night. Right now. It's back.

Alex leans back in the chair. He looks worn, but electric. He points at her printouts. "Gage again. There."

This time she's the one nodding. She grabs his old pocket watch and stares at it. "We need to move. Before we lose it all again."

Before we lose us again, she thinks, but doesn't say.

"Yes. This time." He gets up and makes for the bedroom again but this time to retrieve his duffel, the contingency go-bag. All these years, and here they are, packing together. Like they did once before.

"We work now," Maya says, drawing him back into her workspace with just those words, just her voice. She pulls him down next to her, against her, onto the files and papers, with an urgency without any room for doubt or betrayal.

It starts and ends fast. He says her name once, she says his twice. He's already thinking about what they need for Berlin.

It is an old game, like playing soldier. He wears his fatigues, marches in quick steps from the duffel to the bed, filling it with precision. She watches from the doorway, a field general making notes on a map. Her eyes flick back to the room and the abandoned files left like casualties of war. She pushes a dark thought aside. She joins him in the bedroom, downloads the files she's been collecting, before returning to her. She hears him move with less speed now. Less urgency. She sets her coffee on the table and surveys the packing. She breathes a little easier and checks her watch. They have time, she thinks, and hopes it's true.

Alex finishes in the bedroom. He moves from the table to the duffel, dropping items into it in calculated silence. Tactical gear, neatly folded clothes, anything they'll need to stay off the grid. His face is a map of old thoughts. Unreadable.

Maya watches, the tension returning to her shoulders as she tries to work. Not just from him. From all of it. It feels like something from their old lives, like a ghost they didn't exorcise. Her mind races. Berlin. Gage. She can't be sure it's different this time.

They shift positions, him at the table, her with the bags.

He lets her, doesn't argue, and it pisses her off. That's an old habit, too.

"It will not be like last time," he says, like he's reading her mind.

"Sure about that?" Maya hooks a wire to her laptop, gets back to her download. Files spin past. He watches, his silence an answer, and that's a piss-off, too. "Maybe we should just fuck and work at the same time. Save a little more of both."

The remark is meant to sting. He doesn't let it. They're back-to-back now, sharing the small space with too much ease. It takes them five minutes to fill every bag, pack every drive. When it's all done, she's breathing fast. He looks more tired than he did last night.

"Are you ready?" she asks.

He gives a nod. Sets the watch to the hour. "Calls first." Then he leaves the room. She hates and loves how fast they fall into these roles.

She knows he won't stop. Won't take a break until it's over. Until they're over. He makes one call, then another, speaking in words he barely lets her hear.

"They have you on it?" she hears him say. Then a pause before he adds, "No. Just me, then." And he hangs up.

He sees her from the corner of his eye, just far enough away to not intrude. She listens, half-hoping something will go wrong. That someone will betray him, take him out of this life. Out of her life.

More phone calls. "Moving in on five." Pause. A tiny, defeated sigh. "Contact end." He checks his watch again, twice.

He hangs up, reaches for another phone, flicks his eyes her way. "Flights booked?"

"I can multitask," she replies, and she can. That part is not like before.

He comes back to the table, to her. The drive has stopped spinning, and she's more confident now. She's ahead.

"I don't doubt it," he says, his mouth catching a little hint of a smile. His fingers touch her cheek and she leans into it. But only for a moment. They're both back at the screens, back at the duffels, before it can get too far, before it can become something they'll have to deal with.

She hits one last key, shakes her head like it's a small victory. "Fifteen hours," she says. "More if they're sloppy."

"We must assume they are not," he says. "This is not the first time you have tried this." He pauses. "The proxy trail, I mean."

She bites her lip. Doesn't know if he's accusing her of failure or of something worse. She stares him down. He doesn't flinch.

"You might have given up on us, Alex, but I didn't." She breathes fast. Hard. Wants to mean it. Needs to mean it. I didn't give up on this, and I won't give up on him, she thinks.

He softens. Not like before, but it's there. She reaches for the part of him that still wants to believe they can win. They can survive.

They work close, closer than they should. She downloads more files, he takes more calls. Every breath she takes seems more relaxed, more confident. Until it hits her again. Until the memory of last time comes rushing back.

She stares at him, a long, worried silence. He knows that look but doesn't turn away from it.

"You think I will disappear," he says. "Like last time."

"Maybe I think I'll disappear," she replies. "Maybe that's what you want."

He shakes his head, speaks softer than before. "I do not want to work alone."

"Then don't," she says, pulling him close. His body is tense, but he doesn't resist.

She gives him a long look, the kind that takes more than a minute to see. "You need me. More than just this." She pauses, knowing how deep in they are. "You're not afraid of Gage. You're afraid of—"

He cuts her off. "We do this, then we see."

She nods, eyes wild and searching, then she gets up and grabs the nearest bag. She's at the door, expecting him to follow.

"You really think Gage is behind it?" she asks.

"Gage is dead," Alex says, unsure if he wants to believe it or not.

Maya drops the bag. "Then why does the bastard still have a hold on you?"

"Because," he says, looking at his watch again, and there's almost humour in his voice. Almost. "I am worth finding."

He grabs the bag, his hand wrapping around hers, holding it, holding on, holding. Then she's at the door and he's not. She's in the street and he's not. She's all urgency. All defiance. All Berlin.

He watches as she pushes into the rain. He waits for the ghosts to follow her, but none do.

In the quiet flat, he checks his watch once more. Takes the stairs in careful steps. Reaches the street and pulls his collar up against the night. He can feel the hunt. Feel the city. Feel danger.

Chapter Four: Berlin Underground

ALEX WATCHES THE CITY'S reflection smear and twist as it glides by the window, caught in the wet glass like a dream dissolving. Brilliant, but slippery. Much like Berlin itself. The train rocks him back, forth, again, again, until his pocket watch taps a rhythm against his chest. Maya leans her head against Alex's shoulder, dozing.

KLAUS WEBER IMAGINES HE can feel the weight of them even from this distance, their newness a gravity that pulls him back. The fools. A target like Alex can't expect to go unnoticed. Their location is easily found; a cheap hostel where the floors are gritty and the walls are better tattooed than he is. By nightfall, Alex has a phone pressed to his ear, and Maya listens like it's a magic trick she's sure he'll reveal. But Klaus knows this is no trick. "Drei Orte. Vertrauen, Paranoia," he hears through the wires. When he's ready, he'll hear everything.

THEY STUMBLE OFF THE train, bumping bags and shoulders in their haste. The sky looms grey, oppressive, and the city smells like rust and smoke. Alex keeps a pace, eyes alert, while Maya pushes through the wet with a scarf pulled tight around her neck. In Kreuzberg, they find the hostel squeezed between a kebab shop and a store selling knock-off shoes, its sign flickering weakly like a dying insect.

Inside, the clerk barely looks up from behind a magazine. "Two beds," Alex says, breathless, and the man drops a set of keys onto the counter with a yawn. Maya shifts her feet impatiently, droplets forming a puddle at her feet.

"Third floor," he says, finally glancing at them with bored eyes. Alex mutters something in German and Maya feels grateful for having learned German in Alex's prolonged absence. She also utters some unkind words.

They climb three flights on worn stairs, the noise of the city chasing them all the way up. A grey-haired old man has watched them enter the hostel, his hands thrust deep in the pockets of a raincoat older than they are. They haven't slipped him yet.

The room is sparse, functional, as devoid of charm as the mission they're on. Maya wrinkles her nose at the sheets and the reek of stale cigarettes. The graffiti on the walls is chaotic and loud, tagging every surface with in-decipherable names and numbers. It's like Berlin's digital underground put in a time capsule, she thinks. A car alarm blares, the thump of bass from a club down the street. The noise seems to seep in from everywhere.

Alex drops their bags in the corner, grabs the burner phone, and flips it open in a single motion. She can see the tension dropping away from his face as he talks, his eyes coming alive as he listens. First one call, then another. His voice low and clipped, German and English dancing together, breaking apart in code. A name, a location, a time. Things Maya strains to catch. He pauses, switches to what sounds like Polish, but she isn't sure. The door bangs behind him, but the sounds are no competition to what Maya hears through the receiver. She's never heard him like this before, and she watches like she's seeing a stranger.

KLAUS WEBER, THE GREY-HAIRED old man, hangs up at his end and leans against the damp wall of a nearby payphone booth. They're hitting three locations. They are naïve to think that will be enough. His leg aches in the cold. It doesn't matter. They'll need help. As a former East German telecommunications expert who worked on early internet infrastructure projects in the 1980s, he can help. He plans his intercept, his way in. After all, young Berlin hackers know him as Der Schatten.

"THREE LOCATIONS," ALEX SAYS, turning to face her as if materialising back into the room. "Berlin's digital underground operates on trust and paranoia in equal measure. We don't have time for the former, so we'll have to navigate the latter." Maya stares at him, surprised by how different he sounds when he's trying to explain. Alex tosses the phone onto the bed, the exhaustion creeping back into his features. "We need to move fast. Get ready."

"Ready," she says, her tone challenging. She is. He should know that by now.

AS THEY PREPARE TO leave, Klaus watches the light in their room blink off. The rain makes shadows on the pavement, ghosts that slither and curl. He takes a deep breath, pulls up his collar, and starts walking.

ALEX AND MAYA ENTER a second-floor office complex in Kreuzberg. The blue of a mobile phone screen is the only light in the hallway, so faint it barely registers against the dark. A woman is crouched in a corner, typing, fingers moving fast enough to blur into shadows. "Next time, knock," the woman says, a cigarette hanging from the corner of her mouth like a punctuation mark. Her words hang in the air, just as dim as the light, then fall as she nods towards an exit and closes the door left open by Alex. There won't be a next time. Alex makes sure of that. He leads the way out of the building, down the stairs, Maya at his side, running. The street's a flood of noise and colour, harsh and unforgiving, nothing like the rooms where he'd worked for hours to build trust. It took a few lines of code and even more lies to earn his way inside. Alex can't help but think of it all as blood money. They dive into a cab, the driver taking them even deeper into the heart of the city, straight into the pounding bass of a basement club.

"Don't fuck with me," the bartender says.

"Wouldn't dream of it," Alex answers.

Their night began like this, full of stares and codes, but the memory is short. "Die Quelle," the first bar, a blocky building on the outskirts with peeling paint and a doorman who looks more interested in his phone than the patrons. Inside, the air is warm and sticky. The noise swells up, up, and around them. Alex nudges through the crowd, leading Maya to a corner where the drinks are stale, but the information isn't.

They're two steps through the door when someone blocks their way. Shaved head, bored expression, a shirt too tight to hide the pistol bulging underneath. "He here?" Alex asks, ignoring the human wall. The man shrugs but lets them pass.

In the back room, things are quieter. Edgier. Huddled figures trade data over bottles of beer. Alex finds who he's looking for, a kid with green hair and piercings like shrapnel.

Maya watches them talk, her eyes scanning the room, committing it all to memory. One camera in the corner. No windows. Just the single exit behind them. The kid gestures, sceptical. Alex hands him a card. It glints metallic in the low light, makes the kid hesitate, reconsider. Information exchanged for more information. Maya breathes easier as they slip back out, nothing sticking to them but the sweat on their clothes.

The factory's the next stop, a cavernous space with cracked windows and graffiti thick on the walls. Music spills out from the broken doors, an ambient pulse that seems to keep time with the flash of lights from within. They pick their way through clusters of people, most glued to the screens of their laptops, their faces pale and shadowed in the flicker of blue.

Alex approaches a group, his stride confident, and Maya is impressed despite herself. He names names, more cards change hands, and the tension in the room ratchets up a notch. He's making connections. It's all about the network. But can they trust it to hold?

Someone watches them from the far corner, and she feels the sting of a dozen eyes, none of them friendly. They keep moving, each step fast, deliberate, as if to slow down is to fail. Maya counts the exits, measures the length of a sprint to the door in her mind, ready for anything. A kid nods them in a different direction, gives them one more name before they're gone, into the night and onto the street.

"You're crazy," she shouts over the noise. Alex grins back at her. "Good crazy, or bad crazy?"

Datenkeller is loud, insistent. The bass rolls over them, shaking dust from the ceiling of the basement club. The sign outside is barely visible in the dim alleyway, but Alex finds it like he's been there a hundred times. Inside, they duck low-hanging screens and cables, push past bodies packed shoulder to shoulder. Maya struggles to keep up, the closeness of the crowd intimidating.

The bar is tucked into a corner, as cramped as the space allows. "Don't fuck with me," the bartender says when they approach, but Alex doesn't blink. He knows that is Berlin bartender school 101 stuff. They go through the same ritual, code and counter code, suspicion peeling away with each line.

"Wouldn't dream of it," Alex says out of habit. The bartender points them to a door with a tattooed hand, piercings that run up her arm like tiny circuitry. She turns to another customer, already done with them. Maya wishes she could do the same, just one moment where everything feels settled.

A woman leans against the wall, all metal and ink. "A favour for a favour," she says, bored, as she opens the door to the back. They're ushered through before the words even have time to sink in.

It's the heart of the place, just as tense and secretive as Alex promised. The whirr of servers. The low hum of tech. She looks at Alex, his face unreadable, and wonders how he can breathe in all this. He nods to a pair of kids leaning over a bank of monitors. Time to work.

He introduces her using a false name, and she doesn't flinch. Not even a little.

In a back room lined with circuit boards, the kids have names that are more myth than truth. Acid Dreams. Snow

Crash. Excalibur. They move through the online world like ghosts, leaving nothing behind but their reputations, the occasional burst of static. Alex knows how they think. He was one of them once, before the name was just a way to keep his feet out of the grave. Lukas is no different. Bright. Fast. Already looking over his shoulder like he knows what's coming. "I thought you were dead," he says, staring Alex down with eyes that don't stop moving.

Maybe, Alex thinks. But not yet.

Lukas narrows his eyes as they enter. Suspicious, curious. He's lean, wiry, fingers in constant motion over a keyboard, bleached hair half-covering his face. The room feels like a machine about to overheat, packed with tech and distrust. Racks of servers hum and blink. The air is electric with the scent of hot plastic. Maya feels out of place in her own skin, but Alex looks at home in the chaos.

"Who is she?" Lukas demands, sceptical.

"Whoever you want her to be," Alex shoots back. "We're here for information. Not for long."

Lukas eyes Maya, dismissive. Alex speaks up again, short and sure, stringing together acronyms, protocols. Names that open doors in their hidden world. Lukas relaxes, just a little. But his fingers keep moving, tapping out a rhythm that says don't get comfortable.

"Nightshade," Lukas says, shaking his head. "Shit, man. I thought you were dead."

Lukas turns to his setup, the glow of three monitors painting his face pale. It's an intricate web, a tangle of connections that only make sense if you're inside. Alex steps closer, his focus absolute, but Maya stays back, observing, feeling the crush of hardware and data.

Lines shoot across the screens, red and yellow, blinking at intersections like tiny explosions. Lukas talks fast, pointing at each node. Financial transactions. Shell corporations. A pattern of acquisitions across Europe and Asia. His voice speeds up with the rush of it all, as if he can't get the words out quickly enough.

"This isn't small-time," Lukas says. "Someone's buying up satellite tech companies. But not just buying. Gutted for patents and people." The edge of excitement creeps into his voice, a fever that sweeps the room.

Maya's eyes dart over the screen, her brain kicking into overdrive. She sees it—just a flash, but enough. She leans forward, her finger stabbing at a name, the shock evident. "Wait. This one."

Lukas barely glances up. "A subsidiary," he says. "Shell company. Big deal."

"*It is,*" she insists, pushing through the noise. "Gage. That's Lionel Gage's."

Lukas slows, the momentum of his words halting for the first time. Alex straightens, the gravity of her discovery changing everything. They follow the thread together, the weight of it pulling tight.

"This is serious," Lukas says, spinning his chair to face them. "Methodical. They're building something. Big." He pauses, and Maya can almost see the gears turning in his mind. "But... maybe I can... Wait." He swivels back to his monitors, intent, the world falling away until there's only him and the keys.

His eyes go wide, like he's seeing the answer for the first time. "Holy shit," he says. "The registration dates. They match the satellite launch schedules."

"Next-gen communications," Alex murmurs, his voice thick with realisation. "How soon?"

"Less than a month," Lukas answers, and his fear echoes through the room.

The data streams onto a flash drive, the hum of the machines filling the silence left by Lukas's words. Alex and Maya leave the room feeling like a trap has been sprung and they're at its centre. But they're not caught. Not yet.

SHE REMEMBERS HOW HER father held her hand on those long childhood walks home, gripping it tight enough to leave a mark. "Stick to the well-lit streets," he would say, his voice echoing in her ears as they hurried from pool to pool of yellow light. Maya is far from home now. The Berlin night closes in around her and Alex, cold and wet and breathing down their necks. They cut through the darkness, moving quickly, but Maya can almost feel the fingers of the city wrapping around her wrists. She doesn't look back. Alex does.

"We're not alone," he says, pulling her down an alley, the walls pressing in on either side. It's a different kind of dark in here, one that suffocates. He pulls her against the wall. She's about to protest when she hears footsteps, sees the shadow pass by, and holds her breath, the sound of her pulse loud in her ears. The shadow doubles back. Alex moves.

"Careful," the man says, his voice cutting through the damp. "We wouldn't want anything to happen before we had a chance to chat."

The words hang in the cold air, soaked with threat and promise. Alex keeps his stance wide, cautious. He edges forward, ready to move if the older man tries anything. Silver hair, outdated suit, a noticeable limp as he steps from the shadows. "You're curious," Klaus says. "That could be a problem."

Maya follows, her face still flushed from the tension of the chase. "Who the hell are you?" Her breath comes in visible bursts, fast and short, but she meets Klaus's eyes with more courage than certainty.

"Someone who knows the stakes," he replies, his accent slight but unmistakeable. He turns his back, confident, walking a few paces before looking over his shoulder. "You're running out of time," he adds. "Do you want to waste it on another chase?"

Alex hesitates, hand brushing the flash drive in his pocket. "We could lose him," he mutters to Maya, weighing their options. Her instincts are already deciding.

"We could learn something," she counters, pressing the record button on her phone and tucking it discreetly into her coat.

They follow, suspicion a third companion, as Klaus leads them through narrow streets. Maya notices every detail, the way he favours one leg, the dark buildings looming like quiet conspirators. Alex watches for any sudden movement, staying half a step behind. He wonders what they really have to lose.

"Is this about Lionel Gage?" Maya asks, her voice cutting through the night like a blade.

Klaus doesn't answer immediately. He takes a drag on a cigarette, the tip flaring in the damp air, a pinpoint of red that burns fast and bright. "We should talk in private," he repeats, as if the question is unimportant.

They reach an old Soviet-era apartment building. Klaus pauses at the door, his eyes catching the streetlight like a wolf's. "Inside," he says. It's not quite an invitation.

Maya and Alex exchange a look. They're already in over their heads, and they both know it. But where else would they go? They slip past Klaus into the dim stairwell.

Upstairs, Maya feels the walls close in as she sees where Klaus lives. Unmarked file boxes are stacked like sentinels. Tangled cables snake across the floor. It's a bunker, not a home. "He's paranoid," she whispers to Alex. "Or really knows his stuff."

Alex isn't sure which is worse. He watches Klaus, who's suddenly at ease in the cluttered room. Klaus picks up a piece of old radio equipment, eyes it like a relic from another life. He sets it down and turns to face them, taking a moment to judge the risk. Or maybe just to savour it.

"You're asking dangerous questions," he says, finally. His voice is a mix of warning and challenge. "The kind that get you followed." He smirks, and Maya is struck by how it softens his face, the unexpected amusement behind it. She wonders what he knows, what part he plays.

"Like we didn't notice," Alex shoots back, sharp. He grips the flash drive tighter, but he doesn't make a move to leave.

Klaus laughs, a short, dry sound. He tosses a phone onto the table. "That one was me. There will be others."

Maya grabs the phone, scrolling through numbers and locations. She sees the proof of their trip across Berlin, the shadow of it. "This is all from tonight," she says, both impressed and worried.

Klaus nods, then gestures to the files, the equipment, the controlled chaos of the room. "From this week, too. This month. Farther back."

"How far?" Maya asks. She feels Alex shift beside her, impatient, his guard still up.

"Long enough," Klaus says, cryptic. "You are chasing more than you think. But I suppose you know that by now."

Maya watches his face for a lie, for a crack, but finds only an unsettling calm. "Then what are we really chasing?" she asks, risking a step closer.

"Do you care?" Klaus counters, his eyes bright and mocking. "Or do you only care about what he knows?"

Maya hears the word he and realises how easily Klaus puts the pieces together, how aware he is of everything they've done. It's a strength and a threat. "Why should we trust you?" she says, testing him again.

"Because you don't have time not to." He speaks without hesitation, certainty heavy in every word. "And because I haven't given you a reason not to. Yet."

Alex and Maya exchange another look, a mix of frustration and curiosity. They won't know if it's a trap until it's sprung, but something in Klaus's tone, in the reckless confidence of his offer, makes them want to find out.

He pulls open a file box, the smell of old paper and dust mingling with the tension in the air. "This is where we start," Klaus says, leaving it there.

And for now, that's enough.

Chapter Five: The Ghost of Gage

A SHOWER OF KLAUS'S printouts covers the decrepit Berlin hotel room like a ticker-tape parade. Victories, Alex thinks. That's what Maya expects to see when she scours the papers and laptop screens for clues. "Keep looking," she says. Her voice is even, but her eyes make him dizzy. They jump from document to document; tracing patterns Alex is sure don't exist. "We're missing something," she insists. He's starting to believe the thing they're missing is sanity.

"Face it," he says. "This one's a dead end."

Piles of reports teeter around them, a fragile architecture of failed hopes. Laptops glare from every surface, their whirring fans adding a layer of heat to the air. Maya perches cross-legged on the stained hotel bed, surrounded by the debris of their latest hunt. Yellow and pink highlighters litter the floor. She clicks a pen with one hand and scrolls with the other, oblivious to the mess.

"He's alive," she says. "I know it."

"What if you're wrong?"

"I never am." She says it so simply he almost believes her.

Alex steps over a tangle of charging cables, picking through the stacks of printouts. There's a faint odour of desperation beneath the stronger smell of stale cigarettes and curry from the restaurant next door. The papers are cluttered with Maya's frantic notes, lines and arrows stabbing through numbers like tiny acts of violence. Battery warnings flash on the laptop screens, daring him to charge them again.

He's been here before, this room, this kind of moment, and he knows how these scenes usually end. With nothing.

Alex lifts a sheet at random, looks at it, throws it down. "Garbage," he mutters.

Maya doesn't even glance up. "There's a pattern," she says. Her voice is unshakable. "I can feel it."

Alex crosses his arms, stares at the jumble of documents, and shakes his head. A plan? Sure. She always thinks there's a plan. Her talent is seeing connections no one else does. His talent is seeing the futility of seeing connections. Sometimes he thinks they're the perfect team.

Mostly, though, he doesn't.

"Look," Maya says, and there's urgency now, maybe even excitement. "Start with the Cayman accounts."

She tosses a stack of printouts at him. It scatters like confetti. "Now the Isle of Man," she says. Her eyes keep their frantic pace, but they're on the screen this time, not him. "Through the Italian fronts."

"Should we follow these, too?" he says. He points to an unruly pile next to a pizza box. She follows his gaze, groans, gets up, and hunts through the mess. A strand of dark hair falls across her face. She tucks it back, focused, throws him another set of pages. They rustle like tiny wings.

"Maybe you're right," she says. Her tone gives away her true meaning. She really means, *Maybe you're right, and I'm the Queen of England.*

They pick through the records in silence. Alex stops every few seconds, takes off his glasses, and rubs his eyes. He reads the same numbers over and over, and every time he thinks they're different, Maya has to remind him they're not. Hours blur like this, and so can weeks. Once he knew what they were after, but now it's as much a mystery to him as to anyone. There's something they're not seeing, and it's driving him mad.

They've tracked transactions through a dozen off-shore havens and a hundred companies that don't even exist on paper, until now. He studies Maya's notes. Each page contains a crime novel in her cramped, sideways writing. It's one he can't make himself believe.

The silence stretches between them, a test of wills and of time. Alex breaks it. "Okay," he says, "humour me. Let's pretend there really is a plan. Let's pretend Gage is still alive, that this isn't all a pointless ghost hunt. How long do we keep doing this?"

Maya doesn't answer.

"He's dead, Maya," Alex says. "Dead, retired, vanished. In this line of work, what's the difference?"

"I thought I told you," Maya says. She stops scrolling, meets his eyes. "I'm never wrong."

And that's when she sees it. The smile on her face makes him dizzy all over again.

"There!" she says, and her voice is a symphony, a fanfare. "Satellite companies!"

Alex looks at her blankly.

"Satellite companies," she repeats. Her fingers point to the screen like it contains the meaning of life. "Those funds? Look. They're not just moving through shell companies anymore. They're moving through tech companies. Real ones. Real ones dealing in satellite communications."

This time Alex follows the threads and finds them tighter than he'd imagined. He starts to say something, stops, starts again.

"It's Gage," he whispers.

And now she follows his lead. "How *can you* be sure?"

Alex looks up from the records and finds his voice again. "See this? That's his signature."

"What?" She almost leaps from the bed.

"It's him, Maya. It's really him."

She looks at him like he's magic. He hasn't seen that in years.

"He wanted us to find this," Alex says. His whole body is shaking, not just his voice. "Or he wanted someone to. We've been following a setup."

He rushes through the sheets of paper, through the files on Maya's laptops. His old confidence returns, that certainty he once had that the world made sense and all it took to beat it was smarts and luck. It's been a while. It feels good.

"We need to move," he says.

The digital trail is sprawling, and Maya sees her fingerprints all over it. That alone should scare her, but the thrill is what she feels first, the joy. Then she looks at Alex, and he's all focus and determination again, not that frustrated and bewildered shell. There's something he isn't saying, something important, something she can't even guess at. The knowledge puts a knot in her stomach, and she remembers for a moment that trust isn't supposed to feel like this.

The mouse clicks faster than she thought possible. Alex doesn't speak when he works, just points to what he needs and leaves Maya to fill in the blanks. It used to infuriate her. Now it does something worse.

"Here," Maya says. Her breath is coming faster, almost frantic. She shows him a surveillance cam shot. A private airfield. The picture's too blurry to mean anything to her. "Is this—?"

Alex's hands tremble as he enlarges it. They work over the keyboard like the letters are on fire.

"It's Gage," he says. "It's really him."

She sees him hold back whatever emotion it's supposed to be, and that is what scares her, because she doesn't know whether it means he thinks he's wrong again or whether it means he thinks he's right.

"We need more," he says.

They pore over the files with renewed urgency. Each time Alex thinks they've reached a dead end, Maya points to something new, another path. It might have been brilliance if it didn't feel so much like mania. Documents spill onto the floor, stack up on the bedsheets, threaten to bury them both.

Maya pauses, sees another clue buried beneath the noise. "Silent Protocol?" she says. "Any of this mean anything to you?"

Alex is already diving in. She has to skip out of the way to avoid getting hit with a sheaf of reports. He's almost shouting: "We're seeing the same thing. There—"

"Documents," Maya says. "References."

"His work," Alex interrupts her. His voice is rising, unsteady. He shakes the paper at her. "His patterns. He's alive, and this isn't just satellite communications. It's bigger."

And now she sees what they both hoped and feared. It brings them together, and it tears them apart.

Silent Protocol, it says. Silent Protocol.

And beneath that, written in a code she's finally learning to understand: *Der Kaiser lebt*. The emperor lives.

"He's alive," she says, this time to herself. She meets Alex's eyes. "He's alive, and he's planning something big."

"Everything," Alex says. "He's planning everything."

For once, they are both certain.

SHE MAKES HIM WEAR the tie. It doesn't matter, she says, but if it doesn't matter, Alex wonders why she's so insistent. His collar feels like a noose. His face is flushed and red. The flush is from the heat in the Berlin data centre, but the red is from embarrassment. "Consultant," he tells himself, almost like he believes it. He wipes a sheen of sweat from his brow and moves to the side when they reach the first layer of security. She talks to the guards while he stands there, nervous, useless, decorative.

Maya wears the coat like it doesn't hide three pounds of equipment. Her voice has a sharp edge to it, even when she's trying to sound calm. "He'll be handling the software," she tells the guards. Her eyes are bright. "Just a little due diligence."

They wave Alex through after a half-hearted inspection. He tries not to tremble when they hand him back the laptop case. He wonders how she's pulling it off, but mostly he wonders when she'll stop.

He catches up to her on the other side. She acts like nothing's happened, like they didn't just dodge a bullet. His heart is thumping.

"I told you the tie would help," she says. Her expression tells him something else would help even more. A backbone, maybe.

"You learning to be fluent in German helps and... luck," he says, still surprised they didn't trip the first alarm. "You can't count on it."

"The German or luck?"

The place is all stainless steel and perfect climate control, a network fortress in the heart of the city. Employees hurry through the corridors in matching polos, oblivious. The name on the door isn't important. Just another outfit peddling secure, anonymous hosting, another target that won't even know it's been hit.

Maya takes point, leading him through the second security door. She flashes the credentials like a magic trick, like a matador. He thinks that makes him the bull. She lets him sweat while she works the situation. Her talent for improvisation should scare him more than it does. Maybe it's because it's not the only thing about her that does.

This is the farthest they've gone without incident. So far.

"You act like you've never done this before," Maya says. She waits for him in the next corridor, just out of earshot of more guards.

"I haven't," Alex says.

They pass through another checkpoint, his stomach a tight knot. She leaves most of the talking to him this time, and her silence frightens him more than the guards do. She smirks while he stammers out excuses. "We don't have you on the list," the woman with the clipboard says.

"Check again," Maya says. Her confidence is something terrifying to behold.

They check again. "It's not in the schedule," one of the other guards says.

"We'll just come back next week," Alex blurts. "When it's more convenient."

A badge gets them to the second floor, where the real work begins.

He wipes his brow again. "They've got guards on every door," he says. "We're not getting out of here."

"Do you know where we are?" Maya asks.

"Deep shit," Alex says.

He should have more faith by now, but faith isn't what he's made of.

"Past two rounds of security," she says. "Would they let us in that far if they didn't think we're real?"

A group of workers passes them in the hall. Alex moves to the side, makes himself small. It's not hard to do.

"I don't know," Alex says, because not knowing is the only thing he's ever been certain of.

Maya frowns and checks the signs, picks the right direction like she picks everything else, with speed and precision. She reaches the server room first, peers through the window, watches the techs. It's a whole different layer of security, and Alex isn't sure what surprises him more: that they're about to go for it or that he might be okay with it.

Maya pushes open the door, and he's sure they've blown it. But then it closes behind them, and they're inside, and all the fear that they wouldn't make it is replaced by a bigger fear that they have.

She leads him to a row of terminals. A low wall divides them from the nearest employees, and that's where she sets up shop. She's a dealer with a hand of aces, a gambler who doesn't even need to cheat. "You're on," she says.

He's still shocked. He doesn't know whether to laugh or panic.

"How did you—?"

"You should know by now," she says. "I'm never wrong."

A dark-haired woman walks toward them. Maya intercepts her with the kind of social ease that used to mean something else, that used to mean things he tried not to think about.

"We just need a few minutes alone," Maya tells the woman, the same way she's told everyone, the same way she's told him. "This is a little more complicated than we thought."

He watches as Maya explains the fictional upgrades, uses the jargon to hide the equipment while he hacks in. His hands are shaking but his mind is focused. His heart pounds a hundred miles an hour but his fingers keep up. He checks the hall every two minutes. She's not watching him. That's the distraction.

This is what they know, this kind of setup. This is what they live for.

He sees the files, sees the patterns, and can't believe what they contain. It hits him harder than anything he imagined: Gage. Gage has the whole world tricked, and that means them too.

Silent Protocol.

Alex stares at the screen, his disbelief as big as his fear. It's all here, detailed, and he didn't even have to dig for it. It's almost too easy. It makes him suspicious, and that makes him excited.

"This isn't just about surveillance anymore," he mutters to himself, even though she's there now, at his shoulder. He sees her in his peripheral vision. She's looking at the screen with a combination of horror and awe.

"It's a complete digital coup," Maya says. "It's bigger than we thought."

She takes over his keyboard while he stares at the files, unable to look away. His silence says more than he thinks.

"Decentralised," Alex finally says. "They've decentralised the whole goddamn thing. They're creating—"

"A version of VEGA that can't be shut down," Maya finishes.

His voice is almost admiration when he says, "Untraceable. A mesh network that bypasses everything."

The alarms sound before either of them expects it, and then they're racing against time and against guards. Alex grabs a flash drive from Maya, forces himself to concentrate, forces himself not to lose it while she keeps watch. They work fast, and faster still when the pounding of their hearts and the pounding of the alarms are joined by the pounding of feet.

His disbelief becomes something like exhilaration.

"Got it," Alex says. It's more surprise than confidence. He doesn't even look at her; he looks for the nearest exit.

Maya does what she always does and keeps her cool. She grabs him by the sleeve.

"This way," she says, and he follows. His terror doubles and so does his excitement.

They make it through the server room door, just in time to miss a half-dozen guards. Just in time to think they might make it. Just in time to think they're caught.

"Another way," Maya says, already changing direction.

Alex doesn't know whether to call it good luck or bad, but he's breathless either way. They race down the hall and out of the building and slip through a service entrance, running too fast for anyone to know if they're really supposed to be there or not.

He waits to catch his breath before they reach the next street. He doesn't have to wait long.

"Told you," Maya says. She's breathing easy. "The tie."

He knows she means more than that.

THE MAP PAINTS A nightmare in digital red and green, and Alex can't make it go away. The hostel isn't safe anymore. Not with what they know. Not with what they've done. Every satellite shows up like a target, every compromised system a death knell. "Once activated," he tells Maya, "there's no stopping it." He meets her eyes, finds them wide and ready and unwilling to blink.

"He's got it all covered," she says. "We'll have to move fast." It's an old promise between them, and they know they only have days to keep it.

Maya follows the red dots, her expression more alert and more alive than it's been since they started. But this isn't life. It's war. The stolen data sprawls around her, and she combs through it like an archaeologist piecing together an ancient story, like she won't stop until she knows every piece by heart.

"A global mesh network," she says, her tone nearly a question. It's a tone that scares him more than the map does.

She should be thrilled, but he doesn't see the excitement. He only sees the magnitude.

"I thought we had more time," he says.

Papers fan out on the table and the floor, and most are too incriminating to keep. That's why they keep them. They lead back to tech companies and governments and contractors with more secrets than they've ever had. Most of those secrets are already revealed, ready to implode.

Maya pushes the map to the side and finds what she thinks they're missing. It only takes a minute.

"I thought we had more time," Alex repeats.

She doesn't answer, and that's what frightens him most.

They don't just have the server specs. They've got every piece of communication that led to them, every name and signature and date. And, if he's not completely insane, they've got what they need to stop it. But the need has never been this big.

Maya is still too quiet. She flips through pages of notes, cross-checking every detail on the map. They're impossible details, things she never thought they'd see in one place. She's thorough, relentless, and he watches the concern bloom on her face, then quickly die.

Alex puts a printout next to her. "It's not just satellites," he says. The next map is larger, more complete. His fingers tremble as he spreads it out. "And once it's live," he tells her, "it won't just be us. Everyone will be in his hands."

"Silent Protocol," Maya says. "We've got the specs, the infrastructure. We can trace this, right?"

But it's the second thing he hears in her voice, not the first, and that's the thing that keeps him from answering. That's the thing that keeps him up at night, and she knows it.

They both know the truth but refuse to accept it. Gage has always been faster, and their underestimation is something they should have known better than to count on.

"It's already too late," Alex says.

He's pale and frantic. He's pale and angry. He's pale and pale and pale, and this is the first time he's felt this way in years, since the last big job, since the last big screwup. It shakes him.

She knows it.

His old confidence is shattered, and Maya doesn't have a hammer big enough to piece it back together.

"Look," she finally says, and this time the urgency is real. The contract she shoves in his face proves what they both fear. He follows her lead with less of his own than he had just an hour ago.

"It's worse than we thought," Alex says.

"Stop saying that," Maya snaps.

"It's not just worse," Alex says. "It's big enough to take over everything. Once it's active, once it's—"

His hand circles the dots, the systems, the document that Maya waves like a flag.

"We're screwed," Alex says.

She watches him unravel and knows she needs him to hold. The risk of this job, of this life, is something she's never worried about. The risk of this partner is.

"You have to trust me," she says.

"Do you even see this?" He points to a series of memos with a single word circled. He points to a set of specs that defy even their expectations. "It's a decentralised mesh," Alex says, repeating the worst of it back to her.

"And we know where," she says.

"And we know nothing," he insists. He waits for her to tell him he's wrong. He waits for her to tell him what she always does.

It's her silence that tells him.

"He's been building this for years," Alex says.

Maya looks at the map again. Her fear is something unexpected, and that makes it as unsettling as the grid of satellites, the dots on the page, the sheer size of Gage's ambition. She thought they had months to follow the trail, weeks to get ahead.

"How?" she says, and the defeat he hears isn't like her.

But he knows the feeling. It's like him.

"Government contracts," Alex says. "Big ones. We've been too cautious."

"He's infiltrated defence contractors," Maya reads, "and tech companies, even regulatory agencies."

"A complete digital coup," Alex says again. His voice is softer, smaller, with the awe of someone who's losing something precious, something he was never meant to have. He takes a deep breath and puts his head in his hands.

"Is it worth this?" Maya says. "Everything we've done, and we still—"

"You said it yourself," Alex tells her. "We're never wrong."

He's even starting to believe it again. He doesn't know whether that makes him more brave or more stupid than he's ever been.

"What do we do, Alex?" she asks. It's as much challenge as question, as much surprise as defeat.

His decision comes too late, but so does everything else.

"We can't just sit on it, not anymore."

"Don't start panicking," she tells him, because panic is the one thing she knows how to handle.

"We make the move now," he insists. "We leak this, force his hand."

"And get caught with it ourselves?" she says. "He's not the only one with reach. He's not the only one watching."

She hands him the last document. He scans it with the kind of reckless attention she needs from him, the kind that worries her most.

"The full plan," Alex says. His fear returns. So does his thrill. "Silent Protocol was designed to do exactly this. It will reboot VEGA in a new form, something we can't even disable."

Her confidence comes back, but this time it feels reckless. "We have days," she says. "You said it yourself. We have months."

He doesn't see the warning, just the challenge.

"We won't if we wait," Alex says. "Not now."

Then Klaus calls, and even Maya looks worried.

She's never looked worried before.

"Weber," Alex says, like an accusation. "You have it?"

"I have more than that," the voice on the line says. "I have bad news."

"We thought this was secure," Alex says.

"You thought wrong," Klaus replies. "Very wrong."

He turns up the speaker. Maya leans in, her breath a hush between expectation and disaster. The air in the room is a strange mix of anticipation and despair, like their own mix, like something so familiar it's shocking.

"The infrastructure is already in place," Klaus says. "And so is the bait."

"We can't afford to blow this," Maya says.

Alex's doubt flares up and doesn't extinguish. "You're sure?" he says to Klaus.

"Would I call if I weren't?" the old man answers. "The scope is massive. More massive than you believe."

"Believe it," Alex says.

Klaus laughs, low and bitter. "I don't have to," he says. "You do."

"Tell us what you have," Alex says. His tone is desperate and demanding and everything he's kept from being.

"What you need," Klaus replies.

Maya glances at Alex, a question in her eyes, the same one she's always had.

"We'll have to trust him," Alex says. "We don't have a choice." He steels himself, waits for the next bombshell.

"I'll send you a secure connection," Klaus says. "And I'll do it quickly. You have less time than you think."

"What?" Alex's voice nearly cracks.

"Silent Protocol," Klaus says. "Your suspicions are correct. But 72 hours is optimistic. You should act sooner."

The call ends. The tension doesn't.

Maya looks at him, reads the fear in his expression and hates it. She shoves the papers at him and decides as much about them as about Gage.

"Weber's just paranoid," she says. "We have time."

He wants to believe her. He always does.

"Tell that to Gage," Alex says.

"We will," Maya says. "If this launches, there's no going back. It's not just surveillance."

"It's total control," Alex says.

They both say it. And for once, they both know they're right.

Chapter Six: The Cryptographer's Key

They zigzag through the Berlin apartment block like rats in a maze. Rusted bikes lean against the walls, the air a stew of cigarettes and cabbage. Maya sees roaches skitter as they climb to the fourth floor. Alex checks a crumpled note against a dented door, looks at Maya, then at the note again. She grabs it from him, the paper soft from sweat, and finds the right number two doors down. The metal is scarred and reinforced, a fortress against the outside world. There's no handle, just eight mismatched locks. She raps quick, three and three. They wait. Silence. Then a shuffling from the other side, soft but urgent. It stops as they hear feet shuffling on the other side of the door. Then a click as a deadbolt unlocks. And nothing more. "Hello?" Maya says.

She steps closer, tries to listen, but pulls back as it clicks again, locking.

"We know you're there," Alex shouts. "You said you'd do this." He kicks a pile of beer bottles out of the way. They're rattling and rolling when the door opens. His long hair has gone silver. He looks like he wants to hide, like he'd fold himself into an envelope and mail himself away. He tries to shut them out, but Alex's foot says no.

The man looks down, puzzled. Then he lets out a long, ragged breath. The door opens a crack at first, then wide enough for them to slip through. "Seien Sie schnell," he says. "Before I change my mind." He scans the hallway, then closes the door behind them. Seven bolts lock, one after the next. His limp is pronounced, and his eyes are perpetually tired. "Who else knows?" he says. "Gregor? Hans?" He fidgets with a pocket watch.

Alex shrugs, watches him carefully. He senses he's having some kind of episode. Confusion. "A few," he says.

The man gives him a sour look. "Which few?" His accent is thick, his voice dry like paper. Alex nods to Maya, who has already moved to the centre of the room.

The old man frowns. "Where is she—"

Alex cuts him off. "She's more interested in your toys than your friendship." Maya gives the old man a hard stare, pushes past and starts exploring.

The old man runs a hand through his unkempt hair and leads them through a cramped apartment. It's filled with outdated computer equipment, stacks of technical manuals, and walls covered with newspaper clippings. "Another group," he says. "Asking stupid questions, expecting me to—" He glances at Maya, stops himself, and turns back to Alex. "Are you here to buy? To sell? Or to waste my time?"

Maya doesn't look up. "We're here about Protocol Silence. You called Alex," she says.

The old man's fidgeting gets worse. "You have five minutes," he says. "Then you leave."

Maya ignores him, but Alex doesn't. He is staring the old man down, measuring him.

"Four now," he says. His dry voice is unsteady. "There is no time."

He watches them, gauging. When they don't speak, he gets impatient, starts to snap at them, but Alex is ready.

"A Canadian group," Alex says. "Last year. Where are they now?"

The old man taps the watch face with a long finger. "Tick. Tock. Or should I ask Gregor?" He tries to answer questions with questions.

Alex smiles and humours the old man. "Gregor knows," he says. "But he thought you should."

The old man looks at Maya. Her back is still to him. He bites his lip, frustrated, then snaps again. "Talk," he says. "While you still can." He refuses to sit, refusing everything but time. "What's in it for me?" he says. "What are we worth to you?" The old man keeps his distance. Suspicious. He is used to leverage. They wait him out, stay patient, until he nods for them to begin.

"You built the originals," Maya says. Her voice is calm.

The old man runs a hand through silver hair. "When?" The old man turns away, as if the memory is something heavy, and shrugs.

"Before the wall," Alex says. He paces, tries to maintain his distance. But when Alex says it again, slower, his eyes flicker.

"Protocol Silence," the old man says.

Maya and Alex watch him, don't move.

The old man runs a hand over his chin. The stubble is grey. "Why," he says, as if talking to himself. "Why?" He looks at them, suddenly urgent. "Americans," he says. "Always building on old foundations."

He reaches for a drawer, then pulls back. He watches them again, calculating, and paces more, his limp pronounced.

"Not just the Americans," Maya says.

The old man squints at her, suspicious, then smiles thinly. "Who else," he says, "wants to build on old foundations?" His face is pale, but he suddenly doesn't want them to leave.

Alex steps closer, his voice smooth. "Gregor thought you already knew," he says.

Klaus's fidgeting gets worse. He touches the pocket watch and the old scar. He decides to trust them, a little. He lets out a long breath. "Or," he says, "you wouldn't be here." The old man takes a dusty folder from the drawer and spreads it on a table.

"Not yet," Alex says.

The man in the wrinkled suit smiles, the kind of smile that folds like old linen. He opens the folder. Technical diagrams are stamped with faded East German government seals. "Then you already know."

Maya looks over Alex's shoulder. The drawings are complex and sprawling, and she is almost impressed.

Alex takes them all in, calm. "These are," he says, "even better than Gregor thought."

The old man's eyes move from Alex to Maya, wary. Then he lets out a ragged breath and nods. "Not just better," he says. "They're still live." He looks at Alex, harder. "Did Gregor," he says, "also tell you to bring me a heart attack?" He fidgets again. The pocket watch looks heavy, its face almost worn down from touching it. "Americans," he says. "Lazy, like always. Thought they redesigned every-thing." He moves with surprising speed, shuffles through papers and diagrams. He seems nervous, but strangely happy. "Stupid programmers," he says, and the amusement is dry. "The old system is still in place. They never changed the architecture."

Alex is about to say something, but the man holds up a finger. "Wait," he says. He digs deeper, papers fluttering to the ground like brittle leaves.

A small codebook emerges. The man flips through it quickly, finds the right page, then nods to himself. "Then you," he says, "must have this." The man is in full control now. He hands a photocopy to Alex, his hands steady for the first time.

Alex studies it carefully. "Old authentication proce-dures," he says.

The old man is almost animated. "And relays," he says. "And emergency overrides." Maya reads over Alex's shoul-der. Her eyes flick from diagram to diagram.

"A fail-safe," the old man says, and Alex sees it, too. The systems are spread across the table, a web of complexity and connection. "There's a built-in fail-safe."

He is out of breath, the excitement and paranoia racing each other. "An analogue manual override. With physical access." He jabs a diagram with his finger. Alex and Maya exchange a quick glance as they realise the implications.

The old man sees their reaction, and his expression changes. "You're not just curious," he says. His eyes widen. "Someone is actually attempting this?" His voice is a mix of shock and excitement but mostly fear.

Alex doesn't deny it.

"If they do," the old man says, and trails off. He finds another sheet, quickly scrawls a long string of code on the back and presses it into Alex's hand. "This will disable the authentication protocols. For ninety seconds. Then the system locks down completely." They see his urgency, his sudden willingness. He looks like he is going to say more but stops himself. "No," he says, finally. "You have to go."

Maya is already moving for the door, her steps light. She relocks every bolt as Alex follows her, in a hurry. But the old man's hand grabs his arm, a strong grip. "When they fail," he says, and his voice is different now. Almost sad. "The next ones will be worse. At least," he says, "the Stasi had faces."

"Maybe," he says. "They will be like me." Alex thinks he is talking to himself.

Klaus Weber's space is more bunker than apartment, everything on top of everything else. Alex in one corner, Maya in another. Their host in the middle, a nervous sun with three satellites. The light is harsh, fluorescent. He moves in quick orbits, shuffling and pacing.

"Not much time left," Alex says. The man flinches. His distrust is immediate. "Then talk faster," he says. He seems to have regressed.

Maya looks around the room.

Klaus notices. "What happens when they gain access?" He says then hesitates, then moves towards a cabinet. "They don't have access yet." The faded folder says he's right. The paranoia is still there, but there's something else, too. A hint of dark amusement in his voice.

He spreads papers on a table, limps to a chair, changes his mind and limps back. "Old architecture," he says. "You can't believe how much they—" His hands shake with energy, and he stops himself.

"Are you sure?" Maya says. He stares, a mix of suspicion and defiance. His fidgeting gets worse.

"We wouldn't be here if we were sure," Alex says. Klaus narrows his eyes. They tell him everything. More than Gregor said, more than he wants to know. He stays quiet, absorbs it all.

Finally, he speaks. "Impossible," he says. "Crazy." His pacing increases, more frantic.

Maya thinks of the last hacker they met. "The kid is good," Maya says. "You should see him. You'd be impressed." She isn't smiling, but there's admiration in her voice. She hopes this might draw out the old man.

Klaus touches the scar on his leg through his pants and again fiddles with his pocket watch. He seems manic then bombards them with questions. "How far? Who else? Where?"

Alex interrupts. "Calm down," he says. "Just slow down." The old man can't. He shakes his head, starts to slow, and then he's at it again.

"As soon as I mentioned a young hacker, he sounds jealous," Maya says.

"I was their age once," he says, and it sounds like a threat.

The dry laugh. The distrust. The flash of understanding, more like fear. The thrill when he can't stop himself. "It's just a game to you," he says. He sits, stands, then sits again. It's hard to tell if he's talking about the kid or them or himself. His words trip over themselves, impatient.

Alex cuts him off. "Can you help us?"

The old man is stunned, as if it's a question nobody asked before. He tries to stay angry. It doesn't work. He turns back to his schematics. "Yes," he says. "Yes."

The room is in constant motion. Maya looks at a map on the wall, Alex at more diagrams. Klaus in the centre, fielding their questions, frantic. His words come in a flood. "Without authentication," he says, "anyone can control them. If you know the sequence." He thinks they already know this.

Maya asks about power. Klaus is dismissive. "Old satellites. The batteries," he says, "are very small bombs." He frowns, fidgets. "You're playing with fire."

He shows them a wall of clipped newspapers. A small headline, and he gestures at it wildly. "Code six. You know what this means?"

Alex nods, calm.

Klaus lets out a long breath, tries to sit but gets up again, can't stop moving. His interest gets the better of him. "Crazy," he says, his eyes full of excitement. "But maybe."

They draw him out.

Maya says, "Then why won't you?"

"Who else can?" Alex added.

Klaus is weak to the flattery.

"I was their age once," he says, a dry laugh. "Your time is short. This is what you want?" His hands are a blur as he writes down code.

Alex presses for more. "What else should we know?"

Klaus hands him the sheet. "After ninety seconds," he says, "you know what happens."

The excitement peaks.

"What else?" Maya says.

Klaus nods, the thrill of it too much. "You're crazy," he says. "But maybe."

"Before they," he starts. "Before you." He finishes.

Alex says, "Try us," as they slip out.

HE'S ALONE AGAIN, A hermit in a high-rise cave. The air feels thin. They're gone but he's more trapped than ever. Before they, he said. Before you. They might make it in time, he thinks. Maybe not. They're crazy. He's crazy. The paper in Alex's hand says ninety seconds. Less now. Much less. A single light swings, and so do his hopes. The old scars itch more than usual. Like they know something he doesn't. No one else knows. He shakes his head, limps across the room. They're gone. They really did it, he thinks. Left him. With everything.

They won't make it. Not far. Not with that. He gave them all he could. Wasn't enough. He knows. His grip is firm, but for how long? He feels it slipping, like always. They're just kids. Like he was. More foolish, even. That's something. He sits, stands, paces. The light swings again, dizzying. He's dizzy. It all spins, spins. Backwards. Alex says, 'Try us.' Gregor says, 'You can't.' Maya's face when she thought he couldn't see. Disbelief. His face, in a memory. Just as young, just as sure. He wonders where Alex and Maya will be twenty years from now. Gone, he thinks. Just like the others.

The bulb swings like a pendulum. Time isn't on their side. Or his. His pocket watch doesn't tick, but his heart does. It picks up the pace, fast. Then faster. A tune he's heard before. The bulb keeps swinging. A second. An hour. A week. That's how long they have. That's how long he has. His old paranoia was right. It always is. His mind is a scratched record, the same song over and over. He tries to forget. Remembers too much. Remembers what he gave them, then realises what he didn't. Or did. His nerves are tight, the wires from back then. His life a broken tape loop. "Not again," he said. Not again. "Here," Alex said. And took the papers anyway.

Another game. Another kid. Another version of the same old thing. The more it changes. And then, a voice he can't hear but knows anyway. The next ones will be worse. Another job. Another kid. Another chance to disappear. Like always. He'll disappear. They're crazy, but maybe. Maybe. The scars itch again, then fade. Another kid, another plan. He wonders if Alex and Maya know about the blackout of 2004. Maybe they'll make it. Maybe. He's alone again, a hermit in a high-rise cave. A ghost in a very old machine. He hears them leaving, the steps that aren't theirs.

He runs a hand through his hair. It's greyer than last time. The phone on the table is grey, too. And dusty. He shouldn't, but he will. "Always," he said, and almost smiles. He shouldn't, but he will. Maybe. Another job. Another kid. Another chance to disappear. The kid is good, Maya said. "I'm impressed," he said. The light bulb is the only one left. Like him. The power flickers, but he doesn't. He picks up the phone. Sets it down again. Maybe not. Another job, another. Another. Maybe they'll make it. Maybe not. He reaches for the phone. It's the one he never uses. Then it uses him.

The connection sounds like an old war movie. Static and explosions and at the very end, a voice he knows. More tired than his. Almost. Another ghost in the machine.

"Klaus?" it says.

"Not anymore," he says. But he is.

"You're crazy," it says.

But he is. "Maybe," he says, and waits for a new old thing.

"Don't trust them," it says. "Like before," it says.

Before they, he thinks. Before you.

"Like always," it says. He hangs up. Hangs on. Tries to. A hermit. A ghost. A scrap of a thing. A silver sliver of a man. Alone, with everything. He might make it. Or not. Another kid. Another plan. Another blackout. Another blank slate. The scar doesn't itch now. That's good. It knows something. A very old secret. Maybe this time. Or not. He almost smiles. Another kid. Another plan. A hermit in a high-rise cave. A ghost in a very old machine. It goes dark. It goes.

Chapter Seven: Home Ground

He huddles like a beaten dog under the warehouse's leaky roof, DS Bhatti, with tired eyes and a twitchy trigger finger. Every drop of rain thudding against rusted metal is a countdown to something catching up with him. But here they are, and there he is, spreading surveillance photos across a decaying table. A skyscraper glistens in each one, a white tower of power. "MI5's compromised," he mutters. "They're all working for Gage." His voice cracks, and he stops to check his phone, some dark premonition twitching at him. Alex and Maya listen. They watch. Blueprints spill across the table: schematics, security codes, grids. It's all there, 87th floor, just waiting for them to figure it out before Bhatti's jittery nerves unravel. That's how Bhatti sees it playing out.

When the warehouse door creaks open, Bhatti jumps like a cornered animal. His eyes are wild, watching, his breath tight and thin. Rain gushes through a crack in the ceiling, pooling on the floor and lapping at the toes of his soaked shoes. He checks the burner phone again. Then again. Their footsteps echo across concrete, and he doesn't let his guard down until Alex steps into the dim light, Maya a pace behind. Alex studies the space, professional. Bhatti looks past them, at the open door.

"You alone?" He's already grabbing photos, flipping them. No hello, no wasted time.

Alex nods. "Looked clear. But you tell me."

Bhatti lets a breath out, a long hiss through clenched teeth. He waves them over to the table, a rusted skeleton of metal and bolts. They circle it like vultures.

"MI5's compromised," Bhatti says again, his voice low and rough. "At least three senior officers. All on Gage's payroll." He slaps photos down one by one. "They're onto me. Watching."

Maya glances at Alex. "And you trust us?"

Bhatti doesn't answer, just points to the photos. A gleaming skyscraper fills each frame, its surface of glass and steel bright against a grey sky.

"The Pinnacle," Bhatti says. He pauses, checks his phone. Thumbs a text, something rapid and anxious. "87th floor is your target. Satellite uplink, disguised as telecommunications equipment. You sabotage this, and Protocol Silence fails."

The photos stick to the table, slick with rain. Bhatti fumbles with them, spreads them out. Blueprints follow: lines and codes, security grids, a labyrinth of connections. His hands shake, the papers a blur.

Alex leans in, tracing routes with a precise finger. His eyes narrow. "This is current?"

"Was. As of yesterday," Bhatti says, pacing. "They're not expecting anyone to move this fast."

Maya snaps pictures with her phone, her eyes flicking up. "Why this building?"

"Because it's already set up," Bhatti says. "High altitude. Ideal location. They just slipped the new equipment in, quiet."

Alex looks up, meeting Bhatti's frantic gaze. "And these MI5 guys? They're letting Gage run this?"

"They're getting their cut," Bhatti says. His voice cracks like dry wood. "They want control. First VEGA, now this."

Alex holds the blueprint at arm's length, scans the grids. He's already in planning mode, methodical. A professional at work. Maya moves beside him, one step ahead with her camera, relentless in her documentation.

"This gets out, it's bigger than VEGA," Maya says.

"It's a fucking apocalypse," Bhatti spits. He checks his phone. Stops. Runs a hand through hair matted with sweat and rain.

Alex studies the map, the angles. "And you know how to access this uplink?"

"87th floor," Bhatti repeats, the words a desperate chant. He leans across the table, points to specific marks on the schematic. "Get in here. Disable these nodes. If you move fast enough, they won't know what hit them."

Alex nods, sharp and precise. "Then it's over. Before it begins."

Bhatti collapses into a broken chair, the air hissing from him like a deflated tire. He's in motion even when he's still, his eyes darting, his foot tapping. He watches the warehouse door, suspicious, waiting for it to burst open.

Maya steps back, already pocketing her phone. "If they're watching," she says, "why aren't we moving?"

"We are," Bhatti snaps. "Faster than they think. But not fast enough." He stands, checking the door again. "You get to them before they get to you, or you're fucked."

A message dings on the burner. Bhatti's hand jerks like he's been shocked. He stares at the screen, eyes widening with some terrible revelation.

"We need to go," he says, the panic raw and immediate. "Now."

Alex frowns. "What?"

"They're tracking me," Bhatti yells. He's already moving, shoving photos into a ratty bag. His hands tremble, papers slip, the look of a man trying to hold back the tide.

Alex and Maya follow his lead, sweeping blueprints into folders. The rain pounds, unrelenting, but not more than Bhatti's urgent insistence.

"Get to the car," Bhatti barks, throwing the door open, eyes scanning every shadow. "I'll catch up."

Alex hesitates, just for a second. The look Bhatti shoots him is all it takes. They run, into the wet, into the dark. Behind them, Bhatti shoves the last of the documents into his bag and sprints into the storm, a haunted man outrunning ghosts.

<hr>

Rain blurs London into a smear of lights and shadows. They drive in tense silence, Bhatti's eyes glued to the mirrors. He's got them moving, but the noose feels just as tight. Every red light is an eternity. Each parked car, a threat. "That uplink will control seventeen satellites," he says. "A communications blackout at their fingertips." He tosses a flash drive back, Alex catching it, Maya shooting questions from the backseat. Bhatti keeps his foot heavy on the gas and his paranoia heavier. The wipers slash across the windshield, time running out. The world wet and bright, dangerous.

It's a dark red saloon car, unremarkable, forgettable. Bhatti picked it for that reason. Reinforced windows, a souped-up engine. It's his bunker on wheels, but right now it feels like a coffin. The rain slashes down in torrents, drowning the city in noise and water.

"We need to move faster," Bhatti growls. His knuckles are white on the wheel.

"You said they wouldn't expect us yet," Alex says, the flash drive a cold metal weight in his palm.

"They won't." Bhatti swerves around a slow-moving truck, curses under his breath. "But that's not a chance I'm willing to take."

The city outside is a mess of brake lights and crowded streets. A thousand places for someone to watch, to follow. Bhatti knows. He's seen it before, been on the other side of it. His mind spins like the tires on the slick roads.

"You understand what this means, right?" Bhatti's voice is ragged, pushing the words out. "Seventeen key satellites. Instant global blackout. No communication. Nothing."

Maya leans forward from the back seat, a question in her eyes, suspicion. "And they're using this to control what, exactly?"

"Everyone." Bhatti doesn't flinch, doesn't miss a beat. "One flip of a switch, and they can decide who talks to who. When. Where. How. The whole world, dark."

Maya lets that sink in, considers it. The implication is massive, even bigger than she'd imagined. She pulls her coat tight around her, against the rain, against the cold weight of what they've just walked into.

"And the flash drive?" Alex's voice is steady, but Bhatti can see the gears turning behind his eyes. Calculating. Fast.

"Security codes," Bhatti says. "Access protocols. All stolen from MI5. As of yesterday, they're still current."

"And tomorrow?" Maya shoots back, her tone sharp, almost accusing.

"Who knows." Bhatti floors the gas pedal, the car surging forward. "You use them now, or you use them never."

They weave through traffic, the rain a constant barrage. Maya studies Bhatti, sees the exhaustion in the set of his jaw, the way his eyes flick to the mirrors every few seconds. A man stretched thin, pushed to the edge.

"Why is MI5 letting Gage run this?" she asks. "You said some of them were on his payroll. Why?"

"They think VEGA failed because there were too many safeguards." Bhatti's laugh is bitter, without humour. "They want a system with no oversight, no fucking conscience."

"And if we stop them?" Maya leans in, insistent.

"Then it's chaos," Bhatti snaps. "And we're all in the middle of it."

Alex slots the flash drive into his jacket pocket, absorbs the scope of it. He's been here before. He's ready for it.

"Do we even have time for this?" Maya's question is for both of them, her voice tinged with doubt and the sharp edge of a journalist chasing a story too big to tell.

"Not much." Bhatti checks the mirrors, a quick dart of his eyes, the rain turning every shadow into a potential threat. "But we don't need much."

The windshield wipers whoosh back and forth, a metronome counting down. Bhatti jerks the wheel to the left, cuts down an alley, a shortcut he knows. A risky play, but everything about this is a gamble.

"How do we get in?" Alex asks, already plotting, already moving five steps ahead.

"Any way you can," Bhatti says. "Use the codes. Don't get caught."

"And if we do?" Maya challenges, but she knows the answer before Bhatti gives it.

"Then you're dead. We're all dead."

The rain comes down harder, turning the roads into rivers. Bhatti's got the car pinned, his foot heavy on the gas and his paranoia heavier.

"They might not be onto you," Alex says, like he's trying to calm the rattled nerves of a rookie instead of a detective sergeant with 20 years' police service behind him.

"Maybe." Bhatti wipes a hand across his mouth, keeps his eyes on the road. "Maybe not."

"They are or they aren't," Alex insists, his tone sure, almost reassuring. "Which one?"

"They won't be," Bhatti concedes, but his fingers tap a nervous beat on the wheel.

"Good," Alex says, with finality. He turns to Maya. "We can do this."

She doesn't say yes. She doesn't say no. But her silence speaks volumes.

"The Pinnacle's got a maintenance access on 85," Bhatti says, his words quick, like he's unloading them in case they're his last. "But it's guarded. Tight. You need credentials, codes. Fast."

"We'll get them." Alex's voice is iron.

"They have a rotating system," Bhatti continues, sneaking through an amber traffic light, the rain hiding his transgression. "Changes every six hours. You'll have less than thirty minutes."

"That should be enough." Alex's mind works like clockwork, gears and springs aligning.

"And if it's not?" Bhatti looks at him in the rearview, meets his eyes.

"We won't get a second chance," Alex admits. It's not defeat. It's just fact.

They come out onto a main street, the engine roaring. Bhatti sees the familiar landmarks, the church's dome rising against the sky like a beacon.

"We're close," he says, almost a whisper, the anxiety draining into something else. "St. Paul's."

Maya catches the line of his sight. The Pinnacle looms beyond, a sharp blade in the skyline, its lights like cold stars against the rain-drenched night.

Bhatti pulls the car into a side street, parks in a loading zone. He keeps the engine running, a getaway never more than a second from his thoughts.

"You've got 36 hours before they activate the protocol," he warns, voice heavy with what that means. "After that, it's too late."

Alex looks at Maya, and she looks back. The Pinnacle towers in the distance, its top floors lost in cloud. The countdown's started, and they're already behind.

"We move now," Alex says, determination written across his face.

"Move fast," Bhatti says, the car's idle a nervous rumble beneath their feet.

They slip out into the night, and Bhatti's eyes track them as they disappear into the rain.

THE HOTEL ROOM IS small, claustrophobic, a bunker of coffee and adrenaline. Rain streaks the window, a reminder that the outside world is just as relentless. They plan with the urgency of soldiers, Alex cross-referencing schematics, Maya buried in her laptop. Takeout containers litter the desk, ghosts of hurried meals.

"Maintenance access," Alex says, tracing routes on paper. "85th floor."

Maya nods, fingers tapping like machine gun fire. Rotating codes, she calculates. Guard patterns. The details form a countdown of their own, one they can't afford to miss. The room hums with tension, with risk.

"Tomorrow night," Alex says, eyes on the skyline. Maya sees the certainty in his posture, the doubt in her own.

Alex spreads the building schematics across the bed, paper rustling against the dull roar of the storm. Lines and grids snake over the sheets, a tangle of routes and security checkpoints. He sits hunched, a general in the war room, lost in his own head.

"Here," he says, tracing a pencil across the blueprints, the point a blunt weapon in his hand. "And here."

The room is a crash pad, nothing more. Bare walls. Drab carpet. A double bed piled with maps.

"Two entry points," Alex continues. "Both risky. But the service elevator here gets us closest to the 87th."

Maya barely looks up. She's crouched at the small desk, a battleground of cables and screens. Patrol patterns flash across her laptop, data from Bhatti. She runs simulations, reruns them, trying to predict the unpredictable.

"The elevator's too exposed," she says, chewing on a pencil, her hair a wild tangle from the day of frantic planning. "We won't make it past the first rotation."

"We won't have to," Alex replies, shifting the blueprints, finding new angles. "If we time it right, we slip in before they know what hit them."

Rain splatters against the window, a percussion line to their planning. The room is a hum of electronics, of rain, of tense silence as they think and rethink.

"Maintenance access," Alex says, with the calm of a surgeon. "85th floor."

"That's more like it," Maya agrees, typing rapid fire, breaking through the mess of digital defences. "Two guards. Rotating codes. Exactly 22 minutes between shifts."

"Then that's our window." He studies her face, searching for a reaction. "We take it."

She nods, then glances at the flash drive, a tiny traitor on the table. "And those codes? You trust them?"

"We don't have a choice," Alex says. It's not reassurance. It's reality. "The alternative is worse."

She watches him, caught between the surety in his posture and the doubt gnawing at her gut. "Worse than Bhatti's paranoia?"

"Bhatti was right," Alex insists, his words precise and sharp, cutting through the tension like a blade. "Gage wants this. He's got MI5 on his side."

Maya chews her lip, unconvinced. "And we're supposed to believe we can stop him?"

"We don't believe it." Alex pins the blueprints to the mattress with a heavy fist. "We know it."

The conversation is fast, clipped, each of them shooting off words like ammunition.

"If we blow the uplink," Maya says, her fingers a blur across the keyboard, "we're fucked either way. What if they know we're coming?"

"They won't," Alex replies, voice firm, dismissing doubt.

"And if they do?"

"Then we improvise." He cracks a smile, one she can't help but return, despite herself.

"We'll have to," Maya says.

"We will." He hands her an employee ID, her photo already printed and glued. His confidence as thin as the paper, but she holds it anyway.

They fall into silence, but the room is full of noise: the rain, the crackling buzz of tension, the ticking clock they can both hear.

Alex turns to the duffel bag on the floor, rummages through cables and black-market electronics. "You checked the equipment?"

"Twice," Maya replies, moving to join him. "Communication's good. Just needs a quick test run."

Alex hefts a handgun, checks the magazine with the ease of a man born to it. He slides it into a shoulder holster, feels the comforting weight beneath his arm.

"Just in case," he says, catching Maya's frown.

She holds a radio in one hand, her expression cautious, unsure. But there's resolve there, too.

"Tomorrow night," Alex says. He pauses, looking at her, looking past her, at the city that's already swallowing them whole. "We go in. We sabotage the uplink. We get out."

"We hope," Maya says, and the honesty of it makes Alex laugh. The sound is low, surprising. Human.

"Yeah," he agrees. "We hope."

They move to the window, rain-slicked and cold. The Pinnacle looms like a dagger in the night, its upper floors lost in cloud. A fortress of glass and light, and them at its gates.

"Tomorrow," Alex says, his breath misting the glass. "It's now or never."

Maya watches the building, feels the enormity of the task, of what they've taken on.

"It won't be that simple," she says. But even she hears the determination in her voice, and she doesn't try to hide it.

"No, but we'll make it."

They turn from the window, a synchronised move, two soldiers in a war not of their own making. The room waits for them, the storm a reminder, the night a threat. The countdown is loud and clear. But so are they.

Chapter Eight: Ambush

THE STREET'S A MIRROR of rain and night. Alex swipes his phone. Another photo of a coffee cup, their tenth in an hour. It's enough to make them look normal. Enough to keep the baristas off their backs. But no phone camera in the world has a lens like that.

"Just a bunch of rich bastards who don't want to walk," Alex says. The lobby across the street is as bright as daylight. "Limos, drivers. Are you getting this?"

Maya aims her phone at the glass-walled entry, peering through her hair to watch the display. Six men in thousand-pound suits stroll to the elevator bank. "Pathetic," she says. "And no, you're not. They are."

The light reflects hard off the polished wood tables, and she squints against it, lifting her paper cup for cover. Alex swipes his phone again. This time the picture's of the skyscraper. The resolution is obscene.

They're young, dressed the part, blending in. To anyone watching, they could be mature students. They could be tourists, wasting time between tube stops. They could be any of the dozens of strangers huddling against the autumn wet in the coffee shop. Backpacks, trainers, hipster knit caps. Alex leans across the small round table, watching Maya watching the display. "Is this a dry run for retirement?" he says. "Or are you just hungry?" The paper bag is open between them, and he pushes it toward her. A single croissant.

The radio cuts through the shop's speakers. Weather and traffic and government press releases. Just enough to cover their voices. "I want them to forget we're here," Maya says. She nods at the greasy-faced kid behind the counter, then takes a deliberate bite.

"Are you even looking at this?" Alex turns his phone, and she moves in closer. A stack of electronic equipment and a maze of cables on the skyscraper's roof. All clearly visible on Google Earth.

"Fancy," she says. "Satellite uplink?"

"Uh huh. Somebody wants to make sure they're never offline. Or off-grid."

Maya wraps her mouth around another bite. "What do you want to bet," she says, "the entry points are this pretty?"

The front of the shop is glass from knee-high to ceiling. It bows out toward the street like a fishbowl, inviting people to watch and be watched. Maya shifts in her chair, breaking up the silhouette. Two girls giggle over espressos at the next table, and a man in a too-big coat pounds away on a laptop in the corner. Nobody pays them any mind.

"Lobby is easy," Alex says. "Showpiece. Once we're past it—"

"Once we're past it," Maya interrupts, "we're where? Ten security barriers up?"

"Tops," Alex says. "You know how these types think."

She doesn't answer. Not right away. Instead, she leans back, touching her stomach, then turning slightly toward the windows. It's a nervous habit. It's saved them before. "Heads up," she says. She reaches across the table, aiming Alex's phone, repositioning it toward the kerb. A long black SUV idles there. Fresh wax. Tinted windows.

Maya shoots another photo. "Package?"

"Looks that way." Three men emerge from the vehicle. They're quick, scanning the block with deliberation, with precision, before moving into a tight, protective formation.

Alex is on his feet before Maya can stop him. "Shit," he says. "We've been made."

There's no warning, nothing but the sense of unease and then the split-second shock. Gunfire rips into the windows, spraying glass and café art and wood laminate into the air like confetti. One of the girls screams, too high and fast, and the sound shatters with the glass. A beat behind, other voices join her. Coffee cups spill. People tumble from their chairs.

A bullet zings through the table where Alex and Maya are sitting, another into the wall just above them. There's no cover, no time. They dive, throwing a table onto its side. Wood, metal, a quarter-inch of insulation. "This won't hold!" Alex yells.

Maya nods, staying low, scrambling. She pulls a toddler to safety, scooping him up before he's trampled, before he's left behind. His mother crawls toward them, a blur of panicked eyes and bobbed red hair, arms outstretched. They push the pair of them into the kitchen, then dive for another table as bullets shower the floor behind them. Alex grits his teeth, desperate. Another volley of gunfire. The rounds are hollow-points, low-velocity, illegal for civilians but not for these guys. The professional ones.

"Not regular security," he shouts. "Pros. Killers."

He looks up, takes it in. The devastation, the chaos. Blood and coffee swirl across the shop's polished concrete floors. The man in the big coat gasps from under a mess of glass and broken porcelain. Everybody else has cleared out or ducked for cover, but that won't last. The killers will come inside to finish the job. The doors are all but unguarded. Alex sees their moment, the split-second window before they're caught. He hauls Maya from behind their barricade. A calculated risk. Another burst of gunfire, just off-target.

"We've got one shot," he says, eyes on the path to the back. It's open but it won't stay that way. "Go."

They kick the back door open, but Alex and Maya don't stop moving. Out into the alley. Into the night. Into cold and wet. The air is like metal, like ice. It stings their lungs. "Faster!" he shouts, pulling her along, not even trying to be quiet. She shoots a glance behind them. A mistake. The killers are close, out the door before it shuts, their flashlights raking the brick and pavement. The alley is a concrete ravine, a grave. Closed in. Dead-end. Not an option. Maya shoves Alex through an unmarked door and into a hallway of naked bulbs and half-painted walls. An office building. Maybe. Maybe not.

"Shit," he says. "Where?" His eyes are wide. This is her world, the underworld, and now they're not even talking about the same thing.

"Who cares?" she says, pulling him with her. "Just run!"

The back halls are long and empty, designed to be efficient and cheap. But Alex and Maya, they've always been better with systems. They slip through a glass door and find themselves on a manufacturing floor. Or a warehouse delivery area. They don't know, they don't care, but it has more exits and that's all they need. It's a hasty web of offices, access hatches, no windows, a mezzanine, and bright lights overhead. They don't pause to take it in. It's not wired yet for alarm systems or cameras, so they get out undetected, kicking through a back entrance and past an empty security shack, the shouts of their pursuers echoing in the distance, fading for now. But Alex knows they're not alone.

"They're pros, alright," he says.

Their footsteps slap and scrape, and they're back in the night. Back in the cold. "Out this way," he says, cutting a sharp right and leading her into the warren of old warehouses, storage facilities, overgrown car parks and alleyways.

They cross a yard of shattered concrete and broken chain link fence, and the sky hangs low and hard over them. A chopper. It could be. Or it could be thunder, he thinks. London always feels like this. "Stay with me," he shouts, outpacing her.

The dim shapes of delivery bays and trucks, the trail of cardboard and litter, the industry of a half-dead neighbourhood spring up around them. Alex is fast, always faster, and now the only sound is their breathing, and the blood in their ears, and the whirring thud of what might be rotors.

"I'm here," Maya shouts, catching up. They don't have time to argue, but she gives him *that look* anyway, defiant. "Who's losing who?"

No chance to reply. The night is cold but it's full of sudden noise, sudden heat. He turns and drags her between buildings, instincts taking over again. Ducking into tight corners, he sees the way out, a way through, all options at once. That's his world. He knows what he's doing. Losing tails is what he's trained for.

They make it to a main street, then onto a side one, then deeper, past closed pawn shops and electronics dealers and battered garages, into the twisted arteries of a part of the city no one lives in. Abandoned shop fronts. Abandoned homes. It's a system too. Everything is. Every urban landscape is. Maya knows it too, maybe better.

The red dot of a cigarette flares to life in a basement window. "This way," she shouts, taking the lead, taking them through an archway into a damp corridor between crumbling flats.

Back through it all, back into a sprawl of narrow alleys, back into the night, their breath still hot and raw in the frozen air. "They'll come around," she says, moving like she knows. Like it's all mapped out. "Cut us off if we don't—" She can't say where they are now, just what it's like, but they're far enough and tangled enough that Alex gives her credit.

That's when the guns go off again, a long burst this time. The loudness is almost more than the bullets, the noise of it chasing them. He grabs her arm and they dive behind the burnt-out shell of a car, a patch of sodden earth, the only cover.

Maya is on her stomach, crawling through what's left of a muddy green blanket. "Told you," she says.

There's no time for a response. The mercenaries are fast. *Are they mercenaries? MI5 people on the take or even SAS?*

No, can't be the SAS, Alex thinks, *we'd be dead by now*. Whoever they are, they are splitting up to box them in. One stays at the end of the alley. The other two charge forward, loose formation, but not sloppy. Never sloppy. They've done this before, cutting left and right and taking control of the situation. That's not supposed to happen, not against him.

Alex gets to his feet and helps her up, clutching his side as if it hurts, and it does, but only his pride. A burst of rapid fire snaps against brickwork. Against dumpsters. Against dark and wet and air and night. Then they're out again, running through chain-link gates that clatter like death behind them.

"Not a word," she says. She glances over her shoulder and grabs his arm, not letting go, dragging him with her. "Not a word, Alex."

Another street and more side alleys. Dark but not dead, filled with the smells of spice and steam and sweat. A light. Another. Orange. Red. Blinking neon. In the middle of nowhere. In the middle of everything. The restaurant district. They spill into it, into stalls and vendors and warmth, and the food is fast and the crowd is faster. No time for pleasantries. No time for excuse me. No time for anything except the blur of colours and the sting of spices and the jostle of the early evening market.

The action stops and starts, always shifting. They break through clusters of students, clusters of workers, everyone thinking only of their next move. People stream from all sides. The chaos of it is perfect, organised. But there's an order to it, and that's how Alex and Maya work. The lines are improvised, nothing is drawn, but they're made with an urgency that feels official. The young men in suits, older men in beards. The girls in plaid skirts. The women in headscarves. It's all choreography. It's all improvisation. There's no need to push or shove or say a thing, so they don't. They weave through the haphazard symmetry, back-to-back, between shoppers, and Alex doesn't care about the way Maya takes the lead, the way she's leading him now. But there's something—an undercurrent, a pulse—that makes him pull her to the right. Off course. Off route. He knows it's the right move.

This is what he does, tracking patterns and setting new ones, but Maya doesn't even break her stride. "Are you crazy?" she shouts. It's loud. Too loud. But so is everything.

Another corner. Another line of street food vendors. Freshly grilled mackerel. Sweet bean pancakes. Falafel. More crowds, bigger. Then less crowds, smaller. Smaller still. Then too small. Alex takes a breath, a single gasp of what he thinks is relief, and that's when he sees them, the killers, still too close. "Get down," he says.

Maya keeps moving, doesn't even look at him. She's running blind. Or maybe she's not, maybe he's missing it, but either way they don't stop. Her way this time. He watches the shifts of her shoulder blades, the swings of her arms, like wings, and that's what he follows. They duck into a building, abandoned, wide open and safer than the market. It's Maya's world, unplanned but not unsafe, and maybe she's right, maybe it's better this way. He can hear her now, her breathing. His breathing. Her heart. His. The crackling reports of radios are louder.

They slip through the first floor, the second, taking stairs and taking their chances, catching breaths where they can. The windows are broken, open to the street and to everything. "This isn't even close to over," she says, throwing him another look.

A brick bounces down the stairs, sounds like a grenade. No explosions. Not yet. She rolls her eyes. "Wasn't me."

It keeps rolling, deeper, toward the second-floor landing. They see a glimpse of their killers. Moving in. Systematic. Professional. But this time the suddenness isn't a surprise.

"Here," he says, through the tangled mess of wall and plaster and steel girders.

"Just when I thought we—"

"Here," he shouts again, more desperate. They think they're clear, almost, and then there's more noise, different noise, not gunfire and not close, but something else. Footsteps? Boots? The crackling of old electricity?

"Just when," she starts again, but the words die off and the bullets start up.

Four floors, three pursuers, two options, and not a second to think about them. It's faster than that. Alex and Maya round a corner, any corner. They have a lead but not for long, not with these killers. Pros. Trained. One goes left, one goes right, the last one behind, tighter than before, closing in, corralling. That leaves up or down. The street level might be safer. Might not. The stairwell is concrete and noise. There's no time to plan. No time to disagree. They start for the roof.

The stairway is a funnel, a chute. It might as well be a grave. Alex gets them out of it, taking them through another door, across the third floor. It buys them a few seconds. But not enough. Maya's world, the underworld, is new to him, but not so new he doesn't understand the tactics. They'll trap them. It's inevitable. He sees the split-second flash of doubt, the micro-expression of hesitation, then it's gone. He can't hesitate too, so he doesn't. "Up," he says. "Trust me." They move, but the hesitation lingers like an echo.

It's their first mistake, taking time to second guess, and it's a bad one. That's all the killers need. Maya doesn't like the corner, doesn't like how tight the net is, but she takes it anyway. A corner is better than an end, she thinks, better than a coffin.

She stops and turns, catches Alex by surprise. "Give me sixty seconds," she says, breathless.

"I'm not leaving you!" He knows how it sounds but it's too late. He's already said it. The problem isn't leaving. The problem is losing her.

"Don't be stupid," she shouts. "Go." There's no time to talk. No time to trust. She pushes him, and he goes.

They've always had different plans. They always will. Alex disappears around the corner, one option out of two, and she waits for the rest of them. The rest of everything.

It happens fast. So fast she doesn't know if she can pull it off, and that's never how it's supposed to work, but she has no choice. There's only so many things to think about when your life is on the line, and thinking is how Maya stays alive. The seconds are longer than her breath, so she starts counting it too. Five, four, three, and there's one of the killers already. Close. Closer than she wants. He doesn't know she's around the corner until he's around the corner, and by then the bricks are flying and he's flat on his face, blind and maybe unconscious. Maybe not. One option out of two. No time to check. Two more to go. Two more, or maybe one, maybe less, but it doesn't matter. She's not waiting to find out. She moves.

Her instincts are better than anyone gives her credit for, and by the time the second killer comes after her she's taken three lefts and one right and has half a floor on him. More than she expected, less than she hoped. Enough to let her out of the building alive. She likes it that way. Two options and no time to think. Then one option, because the other kills you. The echo of the gunshots reach her, getting closer, but she's long gone, three floors away and through an unmarked door, the voices of her pursuers already fading. They're not fast enough for Maya, not if she knows what to expect. And she always knows.

Alex doesn't. He knows too much and not enough. That's his curse. He runs. Runs the way she told him to. Runs and leaves her, because she told him to do that too. The stairway is another dead end, and he knows it, another coffin, another trap, but what if she's wrong? *This time? What if she's right? Alex. Alex, always Alex, never where he should be.*

The guns are closer now, but Maya isn't. They split him from her like a wedge, and that's when it starts to feel real, starts to feel planned, when he thinks he's smarter than that, smarter than everything. But that's the way of it. That's always the way. His second, last-second decision is like a life, a universe, an ending. The radio he found is tight in his hand. A second, a single second. It's enough to tune in, enough to understand that this time he's not the smartest. They're not confused or careless. They know. More than he thinks. He lets the implications sting him, slows down to let them sting less, and there's a gunshot that's too close. A mistake that close would normally kill him. Instead, this time, it saves him. He learns it later. He always does.

What's killing them now is space. Time. The lack of it. But it's not killing Alex and Maya yet. The longer they have the more they lose. He can't keep track, can't keep up. First, she was ahead, then behind, now ahead again. That's how it goes. How she goes. His plans are too big for her. Maybe. But the two of them, their plans are never the same.

"Still alive?" he asks, already out of breath. It makes him smile when he says it, when he sees her. But only a little. Not too much. She doesn't smile back. Not even a little. She runs like she thinks she must. And maybe she does.

One last corner. That's all they need. One more blind sprint and it gets them to the last option, the one Alex knew had to be there. It's wide open, maybe too open, and so is everything around it. They're on the rooftop. They see it now, see the space they need, the time they don't have. Alex points to the crane. Then to Maya. Then to the gap. She's faster, so fast it's going to get her killed, but she stops for the second it takes to process the options. They're not all bad. Some of them might work. One. Maybe.

The scarf, the belt, the leap across. They cross. Cross fire. Fire at will. Like will is the only thing they need, the thing they can afford. Alex stays alive longer than that. The bullets don't have the urgency they need, but Alex and Maya do. That's why they make it across, not alive, not dead, but on the line. The zipline. Can it save them? Or does it get them killed.

The swing from the crane and the swing from the weapon. Fire, and gunfire. One will hit, one will miss, but Alex doesn't care. He can't. Not if he's going to make it. He just goes, and that's enough. His hand, his grip, his hope. Not hope. Desperation. He holds on to the improvised line and prays it holds like Maya holds on to him. This time he doesn't let her get ahead. Not like before. Not like again.

More than close. Close doesn't count this time. Neither do the bullets. They whine past, one option, one alternative, but they make it and the killers don't. The killers don't. That's what's different. That's what's the same. This time it's Maya's plan too. She's fast, so fast she should be gone, but she's not. They land together, just as hard and just as rough. She doesn't let him go, doesn't say a thing, just keeps on with him. Together.

Then they're off. Another building. Another chase. Another dive into another stairwell, a fire exit this time. Almost more than they can take. Almost more than their hearts and lungs can take, but they must. "This way," he shouts, and she believes it now. More than ever.

They hit the streets, and the streets hit back. It's still cold. Still night. Still wet. But it doesn't slow them down, and that's enough for them, more than enough for them. Just when they think they're clear, just when they think they've got away, it happens. Just like it always happens. The guns again. The rounds again. The trap again. It never changes. It never stays the same.

When they make it to the underground, the empty station and the tiled walls and the promise of daylight on the other end, it starts to feel less like an ending. Less like a beginning too. It starts to feel like nothing except what it is, and what it is, is a mistake.

"I can't believe it," Maya says. "How did they—?"

"Military," Alex interrupts. The word is hard for him to get out. Like a bullet. "We should have guessed."

They sit on a bench with cold steel legs. "Gage has resources. But this?" She holds the radio he found. Military grade. It's a trophy, a prize, a thing that reminds them they're in the middle of something too big.

"Not just resources," Alex says. "Connections. Partners. Allies." He rubs his side, his ribs. His hair is matted. Blood? Sweat? He doesn't know.

"This," Maya says, "changes everything." They share a look, then share another.

"Not the target," he says. "The target never changes." His mouth is dry, and so is hers. Their backs are against the tiles, their hearts are on the line. This time together. Together.

"Then we hit them back," she says. Not a question. Not a doubt. "And hard."

Chapter Nine:
Revelations

They smash through the door, slamming it behind them, dragging their battered bodies across the filthy warehouse floor. Like soldiers falling back under fire. Like hunted animals, darting for cover. Dust and blood coat her skin, and Maya wipes the cut above her eye, staring at the red streak. It seems to light a fuse. She's up, full of fight, as Alex checks exits, secures their safety with mechanical calm. Dim light filters through broken windows, slashing the darkness, casting angular shadows. He takes too long. She shoves him against a wall.

"No more lies." Her voice shakes, fury and fear fused. "Who are you really? What is Nightfall?" His jaw ticks, his eyes flick to the door, like he's calculating a way out. His hands twitch, reaching for a weapon that isn't there.

Their breathing echoes, harsh and ragged, mixing with the clang of a distant train. She paces, prowling. She's not letting this go. He watches, a caged look about him, calculating the odds, watching his exit, but her rage pins him there. Trapped.

Maya's mind races, flipping between their narrow escape and the lies piling up like bodies. Like the bodies he never warned her about. She touches her face again, winces. Blood smears her hand, thick and wet, but she's more pissed than hurt. This time, at least. Her eyes lock on Alex, who's now circling back toward her, thinking he's got space to talk. He doesn't.

"Got them all?" she snaps, tone jagged as the shards of glass above. She already knows the answer.

"At least two more teams," he says, his voice steady, almost detached, like he's reading inventory. "But we have time."

She shakes her head, incredulous. "Time?" Her anger flares again. "You think this is about time?"

Maya kicks a dented barrel out of her path, sending it rolling across the concrete. Clang. Clang. She looks at Alex, measuring him, not bothering to hide her suspicion, her rage. The silence stretches, a thin wire pulled tighter and tighter, waiting to snap. She's not waiting anymore. She charges.

They're toe-to-toe, the air crackling with what's left unsaid. His eyes search hers, looking for something that's not there. Trust, maybe. Or fear. His fingers curl and uncurl, like he's itching to run but can't decide which direction.

"Nightfall." The word lands heavy, accusation and demand rolled into one.

His mouth opens, nothing comes out. He flinches as she punches the wall next to him. Dust rains down like confetti at a funeral.

"This time, it's my face," she says, jabbing a finger at her own. "Next time—"

"There won't be a next time," Alex cuts in, his voice like gravel.

"Damn right," Maya spits back, seething. "But not because of you." Her words hang there, a challenge and a threat, daring him to make his move. He doesn't.

His shoulders slump a fraction. It's an opening. She sees it. Moves in for the kill.

"We're sitting ducks," she says, the volume cranked up to eleven. "How did they even know where we were? *How—Alex?*"

The way she says his name is a slap. He feels it. She sees that, too. She presses on.

"What is Nightfall?" she repeats, slower this time, her anger twisting into something darker, more desperate.

His silence speaks louder than words, and she knows it. The look in his eyes is the same one from the alley, when they were ambushed. Helplessness pretending to be control. His hands flex again, empty. A reminder. He's not calling the shots here, not anymore.

"You going to tell me?" she asks, quieter now but no less dangerous. "Or do I have to wait for the bullet points?"

She's leaning into him, crowding his space. He feels it, stifling and suffocating, forcing him into a corner he's been in before but thought he'd left behind. His jaw tightens again, and his eyes do another scan, the exits still blocked by Maya and the truth she won't let him escape.

"This isn't going away," she says, her words final, like a judge's gavel. "You want out? Fine. But first, I want answers."

She steps back, the smallest concession, a crack in the stalemate, just wide enough for him to see a way through it. He knows she's not bluffing, and it shakes something loose inside him. He hates the feeling, raw and exposed, but not as much as he hates the feeling of her waiting for him to say something she can actually believe.

His turn to speak. To confess. Or not.

Alex crumples, slides down a rusted container. A beaten man, cornered by truth. Cornered by her. "We thought it was a security protocol," he says. "Not a weapon." His voice hollow, each word a blow. Descriptions follow - government labs and late-night coding, then the grim realisation. Flashbacks flicker through his words.

She's still full of fight, full of disbelief. "You built it?" Her shock a whip crack. "You built VEGA?"

He doesn't deny. Can't. Explains how he tried to sabotage it, how he disappeared. She paces, emotions as loud as gunfire. He doesn't move, takes the hits. More memories spill, broken pieces of his story. Hers now too. She's horrified, relentless. The betrayal like shrapnel. Finally, he goes quiet. Nothing left. She stares, a thousand-yard stare. Rage spent, horror settling in.

He can tell she isn't buying the silence, so he breaks it. Better him than her. His words drag up memories, ugly and real.

"Off-books. Under the radar." He's talking as if she wasn't there. "Operation Nightfall. Security protocols for MI5. Then we found out." A pause, the memory raw. "They weren't just building it for London."

Maya freezes, words hitting their mark. Alex sees it, keeps going, keeps twisting the knife.

"They sold the code." The confession comes quick. Almost too quick. "VEGA was just the first."

"So you ran," she says, accusation in every syllable. "Like you're doing now."

Her words sting, the worst part being she's right. Or thinks she is. His jaw sets.

"No," he fires back, emotion slipping past his control. "We didn't know until it was too late. I stayed. Tried to destroy it from the inside."

"Destroy it?" Maya paces, her energy a volatile mix of rage and revelation. "It nearly destroyed us."

He feels her judgment, like lead in his chest. Doesn't argue. It's pointless. "Twelve years," he says, voice tight, almost pleading. "I've been at this for twelve years... and more."

Her anger, her disbelief, her horror - they're everywhere, all at once, filling the space between them like shrapnel. She doesn't give an inch.

"So, I'm supposed to just believe this?" she snaps, stopping mid-pace to stare him down. "This isn't just some intel, Alex. This is—"

"My fault," he finishes for her. The truth, bare and brutal. "I know."

They lock eyes, her disbelief slamming into his resignation. His memory drags him back, back to the start of all this.

"We were so sure," he says, the scene alive behind his eyes. "Nightfall was clean, they said. Just another layer of security."

"They lied," she bites, her words acidic.

"Everyone did," he replies, almost to himself. The faces come back to him. The late-night promises. The hands shaking his, grateful and greedy.

"They used us, then they used VEGA. But the source code—it was the same."

Maya looks at him like she's seeing a ghost. Like he's the ghost.

"All this time," she says, more to herself than him. The realisation is setting in, settling over her like a slow poison.

"You built the thing that nearly killed us," she repeats, a mantra of betrayal. "You built the thing that nearly killed London."

He closes his eyes, the memory as vivid as the words she's flinging at him.

The labs. Clean, sterile, but the air so thick with lies he couldn't breathe. Meetings in windowless rooms. Sessions that bled into mornings, then into weeks, until time lost meaning and he lost track of who they were really working for.

It all rushes back, filling the silence that follows her accusation. But the worst part is how right she is.

His guilt screams at him to say something, anything. To explain.

"We were just techs," he insists, the weak protest of a man already condemned. "We had no idea how far it would go."

"But you knew enough to run," Maya says, pacing again. "And to disappear."

"We tried to cripple it," Alex says, desperation seeping in. "But they knew. Too big. Too many hands on it. It went global."

He sees her horror, the same he felt when the first hints surfaced. When the full scope unrolled like a blueprint for hell.

"Go dark, they said. Find another way to stop it." He chokes on the bitterness. "Or bury us."

He holds her gaze, a last stand against her judgment, against himself.

"Someone had to warn people. Do something." He runs a hand through his hair, a long, broken sigh following. "Not enough."

Maya absorbs it, absorbing all of it, each piece cutting deeper than the last. "So, you disappeared," she repeats, the scorn palpable. "Saved yourself."

He's numb now, too tired to protest, to fight.

"And here we are," he says, flat, finished. He shrugs, a hollow gesture. "History repeats."

They're silent, two ghosts standing in the wreckage of something neither can quite see but both know is there.

She doesn't look at him, her eyes far away, lost in a place of rage and horror and now, reluctantly, understanding.

When she finally speaks, her voice is softer, drained of everything but the echo of what's just hit her.

"All this time," she says again, a whisper now.

"Yes."

One word, resigned, from a man out of words, out of lies, out of time.

The explosion rattles them like a gunshot, the distant plume of smoke a stark reminder. His burner phone buzzes, cutting through the chaos with a message, a countdown. Twenty-four hours before Silence. The shared threat unites them, an uneasy truce.

"Hate each other later," Maya says, her voice hard, her resolve harder. "Stop this first." Their bodies tell the story as much as words. Distance closing, then syncing, a machine with two moving parts. The image burns, branded on the empty warehouse space: silhouetted in the doorway, bound by necessity, driven by time.

They stand, caught in the aftershock, the distant smoke twisting into the dark sky. A splintered moment, then it's gone, leaving them in the heavy silence. It's Maya who strikes first, shaking off the shock, diving back into anger, as sharp as shrapnel.

"How many more times, Alex?" She doesn't wait for him to answer. "How many more bombs? How many more lies?"

Her eyes are wildfire, burning him down. He flinches, then flares back, meeting fire with fire.

"This is why I'm here!" he snaps, his voice loud, fierce. "To stop this!"

But she's not having it, not this time. "You built it," she says, like she's spitting glass. "Now it's out there, and you can't stop it, can you?"

His hands run through his hair, pulling at the tangled mess. He fights for words, and it comes out raw, ragged. "I'm trying, Maya. I have been. Twelve years."

It echoes between them, hangs there like a ghost. Twelve years. Twelve years. His eyes lock onto hers, pleading for something he knows he can't have. Not now.

"Twelve years trying to make up for it." His voice cracks, just enough to show the splinter inside. "What do you think I've been doing all this time?"

It hits her, but she doesn't show it, not yet. The distance, the hurt, the betrayal - it's all still there, closing in. The ground beneath them ready to shatter.

Then the phone buzzes again, a hornet in a jar, cutting through the fight. Alex snaps to it, flips it open, the message glaring back at him like an accusation.

He stares at the screen, blood draining from his face. Hands it to her. "See for yourself."

The timer ticks down, seconds disappearing like sand through a fist. Her jaw tightens, reading the message, the two words that slice through everything.

Protocol Silence.

"You said we had time," she says, a tremor in her voice, the only crack in the hard surface. She doesn't look up, eyes locked on the screen. "This isn't time."

"Less than a day," he agrees, voice numb. "It's all we have."

It changes everything and nothing. They stand there, the urgency, the desperation flooding back in. Overpowering the betrayal, forcing a new truce. A fragile, fragile truce.

Maya's resolve snaps into focus, a weapon ready to fire. "We can hate each other later," she says, words like gunshots, clear and precise. "Right now, we need to stop this."

Alex takes the phone, hands steady despite the storm inside him. "And when it's done?"

"When it's done," Maya says, steel in her voice, "you can disappear for another twelve years. I won't care."

It sounds final, but they both know it's not. Not yet. They move, bodies speaking the truth. Gear up, gather what's left. Anger shifts to action, raw and focused.

The warehouse becomes a blur, their movements fast, tight, synchronised. Like clockwork. Like soldiers. Like old allies on new, uneasy terms.

Silence thick around them, cut only by the rustle of bags, the snap of locks, the sound of things coming together and apart. They pack the world away, ready to run.

She's already at the door, urgency in every step, the countdown pounding in her head. She looks back, sees him trailing, sees him close the gap.

They pause in the frame, a flash of memory, a flash of the future. Silhouetted by the light, by the dark. The world waits outside.

Smoke and danger and twelve years of ghosts. But they're still here, still moving, and the clock is still ticking.

Chapter Ten: The Ascent

A RAIN-SLICK STREET AND a London skyscraper. Dark. Anonymous. Perfect. Alex and Maya cross, black-clad and unsmiling. Equipment bags bounce against their backs as they move, ducking into the shadows of a concrete pillar. "Same as the blueprints?" Alex asks. Maya nods. Cameras sweep like searchlights across the glass façade, and two security guards pace a predictable route inside the lobby. The two watch, tense and poised. Counting seconds.

"Here we go," Maya says. She reaches into her bag and passes a small black case to Alex. He snaps it open and taps on the specialised tablet inside. "Maintenance system. Simple but robust."

He's terse, almost muttering. "Got it."

Maya raises an eyebrow. "In already?"

"Please," Alex smirks, eyes on the tablet. He waits, finger hovering, then taps decisively. The cameras flicker, then turn to the wall. Blind spots appear. "Move," he says. They do.

With the swift precision, they re-strap their bags and cross the street, skirting the edges of surveillance. They reach the building, slip into a service alcove. Alex checks the tablet again, holds up a hand. Waits. A guard emerges from a nearby door, and they freeze against the wall. The guard lights a cigarette, back turned. Alex signals, and they sidle into the darkened service entrance. It's quick and silent, but the door nearly closes on Maya's heel.

Inside, the dim corridors hum with electronics and the chilled breath of air conditioning. Alex leads the way, following a mental map. His steps are quick but soundless. "You're sure this is right?"

Maya's voice is low, almost lost in the noise around them. "If it's not, we have bigger problems."

His answer is curt, almost clipped. They turn a corner, where a panel on the wall flashes with green and red lights. Maya kneels in front of it.

"Watch my back," she says. Her fingers move with careful certainty, popping open the panel's cover and exposing a tangle of wires and circuits. She takes a small device from her pocket and starts to work, eyes narrowed in concentration.

Alex keeps a lookout, shifting nervously. It feels like too much time. Too long in one spot. But finally, the lights blink out, and she stands. "Still easy, Alex?" There's an edge to her words. He shrugs, feigning indifference, but he looks impressed.

They continue down the corridor, the darkness broken only by faintly lit EXIT signs and the distant murmur of the building's infrastructure. Maya is in front now, the stolen floor plan clear in her mind.

They stop, confronted by a biometric lock. "Didn't plan for this," Alex admits, tension creeping into his voice.

"No?" Maya asks. She pulls out a clear case containing an access card and synthetic fingerprint.

He laughs under his breath. "Not bad for a journalist."

Maya presses the card against the reader, then the fingerprint. A soft click, and the door unlocks. "I've picked up a few tricks since VEGA," she says tersely.

He doesn't respond, but the mention hangs in the air like an accusation. They push through the door and enter another service corridor, cables running along the ceiling. This time Maya leads. It twists left, then right, like a labyrinth designed to frustrate them. But she keeps them on course.

The corridor ends in another door, this one secured with a simple pin lock. Alex handles it quickly, unceremoniously, and they are inside. The room is larger than the others, a cavernous maintenance space filled with stacks of equipment and tangled wires. The sound of a generator is a low, relentless pulse. It's their only chance to catch their breath before the next phase. They take it, each checking their gear.

Maya watches as Alex stares at the wall, visualising the path ahead. He does that, she remembers. Sees things in his head like it's a physical map. A control freak's trick, one he picked up during his old life. She says nothing about it.

"Lift shaft," he says finally. "This way." He moves again, and she follows.

The lift shaft is a yawning void, and Alex hesitates at the edge, holding Maya back. "Two choices," he says. "Fast and reckless or slow and safe."

Her answer is to clip onto the first rung of the maintenance ladder. They rappel into the darkness, headlamps flicking shadows against the walls as they descend and then begin to climb. It's tight and airless, and their movements are loud against the silence.

Maya climbs first, keeping a deliberate pace. Alex follows, more tentative, one eye on his watch.

"It's not a race," Maya says, her voice low and steady. She sounds calm, in control.

He says nothing back, saving his breath. The air is colder than before, the structure a steel lung pumping out chilled drafts with every foot they gain.

Alex pauses, grips the ladder tighter, and his mind wanders back to the BT signal tower. Different part of the city. Different plan. But the same suffocating ascent through the guts of a massive building. He closes his eyes for half a second, willing the memory away.

"We okay?" Maya calls.

He doesn't answer but starts climbing again.

The shaft is endless. Endless and tight. He stares at the bottomless black below him, then at Maya's feet above him. Climb. Breathe. Repeat. She loses her grip for a split second, and he looks up in panic, flashlight beam catching the surprise in her eyes.

"I've got it," she insists. "Stop worrying." But then the tool falls. A clatter that bounces off the shaft's walls and grows softer. Alex counts the seconds until it disappears.

Still no alarms. They exhale together, breath mingling like smoke.

"Don't think I could carry you this time," Alex quips.

Maya lets it hang, her thoughts skittering over the things left unspoken. How he carried her, but then he didn't. How he was gone before she even knew he'd left. It's the silence between them now, louder than anything else.

A mechanical hum rises, faint but growing stronger. "Lift," Maya says. They move faster. Then it's above them, its weight pushing air into their faces. A ton of steel and wires and potential discovery. They press against the shaft's walls, limbs tense, holding their breath as the car descends past. Sound fills the shaft—a vibrating metallic roar—and then it's gone. Neither of them speaks.

It's a full minute before Maya moves again. She pauses just long enough for Alex to catch up.

He wipes the sweat from his face with the back of his glove. Looks up. "We're close," he says, though he doesn't sound certain. The building is a behemoth, solid and impenetrable. Or it wants to be. And there is something thrilling about the fact that they're worming their way through its guts.

She climbs on, following the pulse of a nearby generator. A beat that echoes through the structure and through their bones. Another twenty feet, another eternity. They're both tiring. They reach the 45th floor, finally, prying the doors open with a tool they didn't drop.

The office space is stark. Empty and bright with moonlight now that the rainstorm has passed. It stuns them after the close, humid darkness. They slip inside, catching their breath as they scan the space. Desk chairs line one wall. Rows of computers sit dead and impersonal. Like the place waits for someone to breathe life into it. But no one will. Not this time of night. Not during a security sweep.

Alex rubs his temples, trying to push the pressure out of his head. A tension that's building with every delay, with every threat of exposure. His jaw is set and tight. "Seventeen minutes," he mutters. He sounds brittle. Tired.

Maya looks at him, and there's something almost sympathetic in her expression. "So why are we standing around?" she asks.

They move like ghosts, shadows against the pristine white walls. Alex studies his watch as they slip past sensors. His eyes dart, the focus of a man whose only job is to not lose focus. They weave through the maze of desks, out into an open hall. Windows stretch floor to ceiling, and the London skyline sparkles with unconcerned lights.

Then Maya stops. "Shit," she whispers. A camera, half-hidden, watches like a curious eye. It's pointed right at them. She grabs Alex's arm, and they backtrack, staying out of sight. "You're rusty," she says when they're clear.

"Better than being dead," he replies. But there's no humour in it. Not tonight.

They adjust, correct their path. Maya takes the lead again, and Alex follows. He's unsettled, and she sees it in every move. Every glance at his watch. And every time she looks at him, the same word plays in her mind like an endless loop: *Why?*

"Nothing about this feels right," Maya says, watching the lone guard at the stairwell. The gun at his side looks freshly cleaned.

Alex scans the space and the options it holds. "I'll take care of him." The alarm he triggers screams through the halls. The guard rushes off, and they slip through the door, up the stairs, and out onto the windswept rooftop.

A towering crane cuts across the starless sky. Antennas bristle from the roof's centre like a field of metal thorns. The wind hits them hard, and the cold seems to amplify the urgency. Alex looks at his phone. His face drains of colour.

Protocol Silence countdown initiated: 15:00 minutes remaining, it reads. "They've started early," he says.

Maya's expression flickers with surprise, and something else. Panic. "Can you still stop it?"

He nods, but it's the nod of a man saying what he needs to believe. "I have to," he says. They move toward the satellite uplink, and his urgency is real, nearly feverish.

Maya stands back, giving him space, giving him room to think. The night is colder now, sharp enough to sting their eyes. "Alex," she calls. "Can you?" But he's already working.

Alex fights the main terminal with swift, sure motions. The screen floods with data, red letters over black, and his fingers blur across the keys. Maya paces behind him, eyes on the door, on the stars, on anything but the man who swore he'd never take a risk like this again. She watches, her face a mask of calm, though inside she's wound tight as a tripwire.

Another line of code hits him, and the laptop beeps its refusal. His forehead creases, a flash of doubt. But he pushes forward. "They're piggybacking old encryption," he mutters. "Too complex for Gage's team." He spits out the name like it's poison. "Somebody big is involved." He works through it, his mind processing possibilities, his thoughts ricocheting from agency to agency.

Alex stops and looks at the screen, a tiger frozen mid-pounce. "Damn," he hisses, and there's frustration and awe in his voice. "This is military-grade protection." His phone is alive with digital alerts, all flashing the same damning message.

Maya reads them over his shoulder, not bothering to hide her concern. "Ten minutes," she says, and it's more of a question than a statement.

"Plenty of time," he snaps, but the urgency in his voice betrays him. It cracks like glass. He tightens his grip, shaking hands now steady again. Re-enters code, this time surer, this time angrier. Another countdown clock burns on the laptop's screen: 08:00. 07:59. 07:58. Each tick a bomb that hasn't exploded yet.

His hands are wet with sweat, despite the cold. He's been out too long. Not like this. Not under this kind of pressure. It's a different world, and the rules are changing faster than he can keep up. He reaches for a cable, fumbles, and drops it. It unspools across the rooftop, thin and serpentine. The wind is merciless, ripping the warmth from their skin. Ripping their plans to pieces.

Maya picks up the cable, helps him attach it with sure hands. But her eyes say more than her voice does. She's surprised to see him rattled. Genuinely surprised. "Alex," she says, almost softly. "Seven minutes." It gets to him, maybe, because he tries another pass. And then another. And another. Still no access. Still no breakthrough.

The minutes are slipping away like water through his fingers. "I need more time," he says, desperate and raw. His watch face pulses like a heartbeat. 05:00. 04:59. 04:58. 04:57. Each second louder than the last, taunting him.

Maya sets her jaw, sets her mind to this new task. "I'll make sure you get it," she says. She checks her weapon, eyes hard and determined, and heads toward the rooftop access door to intercept any unwanted guests.

The countdown clock ticks, relentless and indifferent. Alex watches her go, then turns back to the laptop, a grim focus locking him into place. He's losing time. But he's not losing her. Not again.

Chapter Eleven: Point of No Return

Above the city, the rooftop is a god's-eye graveyard of old antennae and forgotten transmitters, everything waiting to be born again. The wind tears at Alex as he hunches over the satellite uplink terminal, fingers dancing, and Maya's eyes dart from the countdown clock to him and back. "Fourteen minutes," she shouts, voice whipped thin. He's not listening, and she's not expecting him to. They need this win. Need it bad. A deep breath. Back at it. Equipment hums with electric tension as Alex's expression shifts from concentration to horror.

The terminal is an island in a sea of cables and junk. Years of obsolete tech crammed together, not quite dead, waiting to be called back into service. Maya pulls her jacket tight. Alex ignores the cold, everything, but she knows it's only a matter of time before it all catches up. "Talk to me," she calls across the void, more hope than an order. Wind snatches her words. On the screen, numbers burn their way down to nothing.

He keeps at it, eyes locked on the code as his fingers fly. He's close; he has to be. She wishes for half his faith, half his skill, half his disregard for anything that isn't right in front of him. The clock is ruthless, digits dissolving with a cruel indifference. Alex leans in harder, frowning. He's in. A quick smile. But Maya knows better than to believe it.

Something's wrong. It hits him like a shot. A spread of red across the monitor. The screen reads like a death sentence, hard and brutal. He fights it, desperate, shouting at it like it can hear him. No, no, no! But there's no budging. This flaw, this goddamn flaw. It was there all along, a quiet ticking. He slams the terminal. A thousand pounds' worth of gear teeters dangerously.

"What?" Maya's there now, her face inches from his. She hasn't seen him like this before. He's paler than she thought possible, an empty paper. "Alex, what the hell?" The hum of the equipment fills the silence, fills her gut with panic. It's not like him to shut down, not ever.

"To stop it," he finally manages. His words are sharp, cut into the wind. "Someone has to go manual."

She doesn't understand, doesn't want to understand. "What are you saying?" The terror in her voice, she can't hide it.

Alex stands back, runs a shaking hand through his hair. His breath is steam. "The only way to disable it," he says, "is during transmission." It hangs in the air, waiting to explode. "It's a manual detonation. Suicidal."

She goes blank, tries to reset. This wasn't in the plan, wasn't anything they'd prepared for. Alex stares at her, waiting for it to click. She grips his arm, a physical need to make him keep talking, make it mean something else.

"Circuit breaker's in line with the main transmission," he says, almost a whisper. It's a confession, a failure. "Electrical feedback—" He can't look at her.

"And you just found this out now?" Anger and fear make her loud. The clock mocks them, a silent snigger.

"It's built into the architecture. Hardwired failsafes." He's desperate, grasping for excuses. "A buffer overflow was supposed to give us time—"

Her mind reels. "You're saying," she starts, every word an accusation, "someone has to be there when it blows? Alex, are you fucking kidding me?"

He meets her eyes for the first time. His are the same shade of defeat as the screens, but there's something else. Resolve, a bitter determination. "There's no remote trigger," he says. "No other way."

Her stomach lurches. It's happening, whether she's ready or not. She looks at him, a long hard look. This is the face of a man about to do something very stupid.

"You can't," she says, but she's unsure whether she's thinking of him or herself.

He shakes his head. "There's no time," he insists. No time, no options.

"Someone has to pull the breaker at exactly the right moment. After the countdown hits zero." The rest is implied, filling the air between them. A life for a life. They both know the maths.

Maya can barely breathe, tries anyway. "It'll kill you."

The countdown blinks down. She stares at it, trying to find the seconds they lost.

"Then it kills me," Alex says.

She's not about to let that happen. Not without a fight.

They stand face-to-face, the countdown clock ticking loud between them. Less than ten minutes now, the wind wild and unrelenting. Maya grabs Alex's shoulders, refusing to let him out of this alive. Refusing to let him die.

"It's not an option," she shouts. "I should do it."

His eyes are hollow, a deep set of ghosts, and the way he looks at her—like he's already gone—is more than she can take.

"You can't stop this by dying," he says, words like a slap.

He turns away, but she pushes back. "You think your guilt matters more than stopping what comes next?" The rooftop screams in electric desperation, and so do they.

"This is bigger than us," she yells, the words swallowed by the wind. Alex steps back, away from her, away from the world.

"I helped build it, Maya," he says, like a wound, like a prayer. "It's my responsibility."

His calm infuriates her. She pushes past him, past his logic and despair. Past everything but time, and there isn't much of it left. "You're more useful alive," she says, loud and vicious. "We both are."

He blocks her from the terminal, but she won't let him win. The struggle is everything she knew it would be, everything she hoped it wouldn't be. Messy and brutal, their lives compressed into one last fight. It's a race to see who can sacrifice more. The minutes slip away.

He grips her arms, shoves her back, but she's relentless. Every step he takes toward the terminal is a step she tries to steal. "I can't let you do this," he says, as if he has a choice.

Her answer is a shove of her own, raw and fierce.

His face, a map of old regrets and new panic. "Maya, stop." He's not used to begging, but that's what it is. Begging for her life, and if she's being honest, for his too. She almost softens, almost gives in. Almost.

She wipes the hair from her eyes, pulls the fight back into her. "You can't just check out," she says. "I won't let you." His refusal, her defiance—they crash together, harder than the storm around them.

The clock won't quit. The wind won't quit. Neither will she. "We need you," she says, knowing how it sounds. Knowing it's the truth.

The charge in the air is nothing compared to the charge between them. She's never been this scared, never wanted to run and fight and surrender all at once.

"Do you think it's just about us?" Alex shoots back. He's a mix of anger and resignation.

The word echoes. Us. The world. Everything they're about to lose.

"I helped build the monster," he says again, and there's fire in it now. The last of his defences, crumbling. "I put the world in danger. I need to fix this."

"You can't fix it by dying," Maya screams. "That's not fixing anything." She gets in front of him, his determination a wall she must climb. But she knows him, knows the burden he carries. Knows how it always wins.

Her anger burns white-hot. His guilt is the kind that eats you whole.

"This is my choice," he says. "My responsibility." His breath is hard, fast. She wants to tell him to calm down, wants to tell him to panic. "Some debts can only be paid one way."

"No," she says. It's a curse and a promise. "No."

The storm howls, their voices louder, the desperation in them sharper than any blade. Maya sees the shift in his eyes, knows she's losing. Knows he's about to disappear again, the way he always does.

He looks at the clock, then at her. There's an emptiness to him that makes her sick, a determination that breaks her. He's already decided.

"No," she says again. He can't leave her. He can't.

"We have one shot," he says. "One. I won't let it slip." He pulls away, towards the controls, and she fights to follow. He turns, faces her. "Please."

The word stops her cold.

His back is to the wind, to her, to everything but the task. A ghost already. "This ends with me," he says. "It has to."

She forces herself to move, but Alex is ahead of her, his will a knife. He's on the keyboard, initiating the sequence. Final, unflinching. This is what she gets for loving him.

The clock is a whip, lashing them. He's closer now. It's under his skin.

Her breath is nothing but mist. The cold, the panic, his resolve. It's all closing in. "Please," she says. "Please, no."

He won't stop. She knows it. She knows him. "Maya," he says. His voice breaks.

He's going to die.

She can't breathe.

They're almost out of time.

The rooftop door explodes open. A gust of cold, a new threat. Bhatti. He's got his service weapon drawn and an unflinching look in his eyes. Maya and Alex freeze, not sure what hits them harder. He sees the setup, takes stock in a split second. Holsters the gun. Moves in fast. "I tracked your phones," Bhatti says. His calm clashes with their chaos, the countdown under five minutes now. "Both of you, out. Now."

They protest. Of course they do. But he cuts them off, his presence an avalanche. "This isn't a debate. The world needs you two alive more than it needs me."

Maya blinks, her mind racing to keep up. "No, Bhatti. You don't understand."

Alex finds his voice, loud and ragged. "The system—"

He's cut short, Bhatti's authority as cold and sharp as the wind. "You're not listening. This isn't a debate. Get out." His eyes are steady, and he's got a calm that cuts against the frantic storm of the rooftop. Against the way Alex and Maya were just at each other's throats.

"He's insane," Alex says, the words strangled.

"No," Maya answers. "He's serious." Bhatti is closer now, and he won't be moved. She can't believe it, any of it.

He's between them and the terminal, like he was meant to be there all along. Like there's no other place he could be. Maya struggles to think, to breathe. It's all moving too fast, and she's not ready, but there he is. And he's not going to budge.

"Out," Bhatti says, and it's not loud, but it might as well be a gunshot. Might as well be a promise. "Now."

Alex stands there, stunned, blinking at this madness. At Bhatti's unwavering resolve. The clock doesn't stop. It's a hammer against their skin, their lungs. It doesn't care if they're ready. It doesn't care about Bhatti's choice, doesn't care about theirs. Less than four minutes now.

"This isn't how it's supposed to go," Maya says, and the plea in her voice, the confusion—it hits harder than anything else. Harder than it should.

"This is exactly how it's supposed to go," Bhatti says. "Get moving."

They hesitate, the world collapsing around them, beneath them, inside them. Everything they thought they had. Everything slipping away.

"Go," Bhatti says again. "The world needs you alive more than it needs me." His words are like fists, but they're too solid to duck. Too final to ignore.

Alex doesn't know what to do. Doesn't know how to accept this. He's at a loss, out of moves. "Bhatti," he starts. The name sounds strange in his mouth. Sounds like a mistake, but he knows it isn't. "You'll need to know how to—"

"Do I look like a goddamn amateur?" Bhatti shoots back. The edge in his voice is fierce, but there's something else behind it. Something Alex can't quite see, not yet.

They're wasting time, time they don't have. Alex starts to explain anyway. But his heart isn't in it. Bhatti knows. Alex can tell.

The wind claws at them. The city below. The sky above. None of it matters. Just this, here, now.

"Forget it," Bhatti says. "I've got this. Go."

Maya looks at Alex, sees his struggle, his unwillingness to believe, to leave. She's not ready to accept it either. "This is insane," she says again. "We can do this together. You don't have to—"

"I do," Bhatti interrupts. He's calm, so damn calm, and Maya hates it. Hates him for a moment. Hates herself for not knowing, for not understanding.

The clock mocks them all, the numbers a taunt. A death knell. They don't have time to win this one.

Maya can't breathe, the desperation choking her, leaving her raw and exposed. She watches Bhatti's face, his resolve a brutal thing. A solid thing. She tries one more time, a last shot.

His words stop her dead. "Some debts," he says, "can only be paid one way."

Everything collapses. Everything is still.

This was supposed to be Alex's sacrifice. Hers. Now, it's Bhatti's.

They've lost, and they know it.

Bhatti's back is straight. His gaze unshakable. Alex and Maya share a look, a realisation, before turning to leave.

They head for the exit, the world unravelling in their wake. The world spinning on without them, whether they go or not.

They look back, but Bhatti is already facing the terminal, ready. The countdown under three minutes. The silence is deafening.

Chapter Twelve: Silence Falls

They leave Bhatti and make the top floor with minutes to spare. Two flights down the stairwell, a clean, dull blast, and Alex knows they weren't the only ones on a timer. Below them, the emergency doors burst open, and he hears a dozen pairs of boots swarming upward. Alex takes Maya's hand. "Let's go," he says, and they start running. Three at a time. Four. They make progress as smoke and bodies fill the stairwell. Outside, they can hear alarms, rain, and the roar of approaching engines. It's not as bad as Alex thought, and that's what worries him.

"Alex!" Maya gasps, her voice close behind him.

He takes the next flight without answering, pulling her along. The countdown has them at four minutes, maybe less. Red lights cast long shadows on grey walls. Alarms echo in his head. He glances back to see Maya keeping pace, breathing hard, not slowing. Her hair sticks to her face in damp strands. She's right behind him.

The plan was fifteen minutes, but Alex isn't surprised it's gone to shit. It's what he would have done. Still, he knows how fast four turns into three, three into two. There's no time to improvise.

They're twelve floors from the bottom, and it's loud and loud and louder as they pass each landing. Up the well, shouts and slamming feet. Behind them, a floor below, security is closer than Alex thought, and that worries him more.

"Maya," he says. It comes out hoarse.

He grabs her wrist, pulls. Five floors. Four. His legs burn. His lungs are wet and heavy. They can't stop. They don't. Three flights to go, and smoke pours down from above. Two, and Alex can taste it. Almost there.

They're at the last flight, and he risks a look back. Black uniforms, getting closer. Too close. Then they're through the final exit, out of the building, into open air. The world hits them loud, cold, hard. Rain soaks them before they can think. Alarms wail into the night. Engines thunder toward them from every direction.

"Keep moving," he shouts.

They don't have time to see who's already here. They don't have time to see how bad this is. Not yet. Not ever.

Maya grips his arm. Her mouth is open, a breathless question, and she doesn't let go. Not when he pulls her down the street. Not when he yanks her into the alley. Not when he drags her behind the dumpster, and they crouch, wet, ragged, waiting.

Maya coughs. The rain falls heavier. They listen. They wait. Boots splash through puddles, and Alex counts six men as they barrel past, soaking wet and angry. He holds his breath, holds Maya's hand tight, and he waits, waits, waits, until the sounds of their pursuit are drowned out by sirens and rain.

Maya leans her head against the hard plastic of the dumpster, eyes shut. Her breaths are slow and deep, but she's smiling, shaking her head at him. She's soaked. They both are.

"You ever gonna trust me?" she asks.

Alex watches the alley, watches the street, always watching. "Don't take it personally."

He waits a full minute before standing. They're not out of this, not yet, but they're closer. One more scan of the street, one more silent second, and they're out of their hiding spot and running again.

"Five minutes," Maya shouts.

Her voice is playful and mad. They should have been out of here. They should be clear.

"Alex!"

They both hear it. A door slamming. An engine. They hit the next alley hard, backs to the wall. The vehicle screeches nearby, tearing through the street. Lights flash. Tyres spin. Another minute, and they won't have anywhere left to run.

"Over here," Alex says, yanking open the gate of a chain-link fence.

They sprint across the muddy lot. It's not subtle, but subtle isn't what they need. Not now. Alex has two back-ups, three, four. One for each plan gone bad. He just needs to get them there in time.

The street on the other side is dark and quiet. It feels wrong. Too easy. They cut through a narrow gap between buildings, their wet clothes sticking to their skin. Every time Alex looks back, he half expects to see headlights, men, guns. Something. But he and Maya are still alone, and he doesn't like it.

Another turn. Another. A few more streets, and they have options. Maya steals a look at her watch, then at him. She's soaking wet, hair stuck to her cheeks, but still smiling, like this was the plan all along.

Four minutes, her eyes say.

We did it, her eyes say.

"We've got time," he says, voice flat, sounding a little more sure than he really is.

They pick up the pace, both remembering what happens when you think you're in the clear. Both remembering how fast the plan went to shit.

"Let's not waste it," Maya says.

Her grin is wide and bright, and the night is wet and loud.

Alex has the binoculars. Maya has her doubts. They watch from a rooftop across the street as time slips away. Maya sees Bhatti's frantic hands just visible through the rain flecked lens of the camcorder they left behind. He moves at the circuit panel with practiced, hurried precision. "Less than a minute," Maya says, and Alex doesn't respond. A brief flash. She counts out five seconds, ten. The system stays up. They both let out the breath they didn't know they were holding.

"Do you think he's okay?" Maya says, breaking the silence.

Alex shrugs, wiping rain from his face. "Do you?"

From this distance, even through the binoculars, the top floor of the skyscraper looks like the glowing tip of a match. Lit up. About to burn.

"I just think—" Maya starts, but Alex is already at the ledge, already setting up. He looks through the binoculars, adjusting the focus, muttering.

It's too close, too soon. They shouldn't have trusted Bhatti to be alone this long. Maya paces. Back and forth. Back and forth. Two and a half minutes left, and Alex keeps watching. It feels like forever before he speaks.

"There," he says.

Maya rushes to his side.

Through the camcorder feed, she can see Bhatti's silhouette, his dark shape frantic against a flood of light. Even at this distance, she can tell he's moving fast. "Looks bad," she says.

"Look closer."

She what Alex sees: Bhatti is focused, steady, not slowing down. He opens the circuit panel, wires spilling like entrails from an open wound, and then Maya understands. "He thinks he has it."

Alex sets his jaw, keeps his eyes on the building. "Bhatti's never done anything like this. Not with so much at stake."

One minute. She's chewing her lip, her nails, anything to distract her from the wait. "He has no time left," she says, and Alex finally lowers the binoculars.

"I don't see him making it back inside," he says.

She snatches the binoculars from his hands, frantic. They should be there, with him. But then, Bhatti put them right on that, didn't he? His actual words were, "Now, fuckoffski!"

Maya peers at the live feed again. She sees the blur of Bhatti's hands on the wires. "He knows what he's doing," she says.

"Does he?" Alex asks, almost a whisper.

His secure phone is out, and she sees him scrolling through messages that don't exist yet. It feels like he's already given up, and she hates him for it. She glares at him. "I mean it," she says. "Does he?"

Before he can answer, the lights flicker. Her heart drops. She grabs his arm, eyes wide. It wasn't supposed to go dark. But then—no. There's still a faint glow. She sees a bright flash coming from the skyscraper rooftop, brief as a blink.

Then Alex says, "Maybe."

The doubt, the uncertainty.

"Alex—"

They stare at each other. Alex looks at the building, then at his phone, then at the building again. The screens stay lit. The systems stay up. But neither of them believes it, not yet. Not yet.

They count it out.

One Mississippi. Two Mississippi. Three.

He must have.

Seven. Eight.

But—

Ten.

The countdown says zero. The screen says it's done.

The system is still up. They're still on the roof. No one is after them. Not yet. Not ever.

"He did it," Maya says, a soundless whisper as she stares at the confirmation message on Alex's phone.

They don't trust it. But the proof is there.

Alex looks like a man who's never learned how to smile. "Don't take it personally," he says when he catches Maya's eyes on him.

A nervous laugh breaks free from her throat. Her shoulders slump, relief crashing over her like waves. They're both soaked, both exhausted, but it doesn't matter. They are still alive. She shakes his hand, squeezes it, pulls him close. "You brilliant, brilliant bastard," she says, voice wild and giddy and nothing like Alex's. "You actually did it."

But Alex can't let it go. Not yet. He looks at his phone again, at the building, at Maya. "They'll know," he says. "They'll know who Bhatti is."

"They'll know he's the best," Maya says. Her grin is wild and reckless. It makes him want to laugh. Makes him want to run. He doesn't know which. Maybe both.

They wait a few more seconds, enough to be sure, and the system stays live but does Bhatti?

They don't even see the phone shake in Alex's hand.

THE BURN MARKS ARE livid against the bandages. "We did everything we could," the doctor says, her voice as antiseptic as the rest of the room. "Now he needs time."

Alex doesn't answer, but Maya nods, puts the flash drive next to Bhatti's limp hand. They make it to the hallway before Alex says what they're both thinking. "He doesn't have time." Then the message buzzes through: "For now."

Bhatti lies unconscious in the hospital bed, his face covered in gauze. Each rise and fall of his chest is shallow, mechanical. Maya leans over him, but she doesn't speak. She just watches.

"Significant injuries," the doctor had said. "Lucky to have survived at all."

In here, even her tone was clinical. Efficient. Like everything else.

Now, a day later, it's another doctor, a new shift, the same words. This one doesn't say it, but Alex hears the implication behind her careful detachment: Don't count on him waking up.

Machines hum and beep, every bit as impersonal as the woman who left them alone with Bhatti. Maya and Alex stand at the bedside. They are not used to this much waiting.

"Shouldn't we be getting back?" Alex asks.

Maya looks at him like he's forgotten something. "He got us this far. We owe him."

Bhatti's arm twitches. They both lean in. Both wait for something more. It doesn't come. "Stable, for now," the doctor had said. "Now it's up to him."

The smell of antiseptic hangs thick in the air. Alex knows better. Nothing is up to them.

A nurse passes the door. He doesn't trust how long she looks at them, at the bandaged man. "There's nothing we can do," Alex says. His eyes are on the door, then the window, then Bhatti, but never Maya. Never himself.

She runs her fingers lightly over the flash drive before placing it on the table. The evidence they'd risked everything for. "When you wake up, this is yours," she whispers. She makes it sound like she believes he will.

More beeping. More efficient footfalls. Maya still hasn't moved, hasn't given up, when Alex lets out a harsh breath, shakes his head. He sees her watching him again, knows what she'll say before she says it.

"One more hour," she says, and he nods, lips pressed tight, like he means it. Like he can make it that long.

Alex doesn't trust anything in this building. The sterile room. The soft-spoken staff. He has the idea that someone has followed them here, and he won't shake it until they're long gone.

In the hallway, a man in a dark suit lingers too close to their door. Security. He acts bored, but Alex isn't fooled. "For protection," Maya says. "You saw the news."

"What I saw was an inside job," he says, just as quiet, just as intense. "If he wakes up, it'll happen again."

She doesn't look at him, not now. Not yet. They stand in the white room. They watch the bandaged man, still hoping he'll surprise them. Still thinking he might.

Alex checks his phone.

"Why would you?" Maya asks.

He doesn't answer.

"Because you don't trust anything you haven't seen for yourself?"

He doesn't answer.

They sit in silence. Maya's eyes never leave Bhatti's face. The bandages. The thin burns peeking through.

"Significant injuries," the doctor had said. "Time."

She makes it sound like time is enough. Alex isn't convinced.

Two nurses stand outside the room, talking low. Their eyes flit from Alex to Maya to Bhatti. "Like they know him," Alex says. "Like they know us."

She doesn't answer.

Like she's never done anything this serious, he thinks.

An hour, he thinks. He can make it.

He checks his phone again.

More beeping. More footfalls.

He can make it.

A nurse enters and adjusts the machines, the IV, anything she can put her hands on. Anything she can control. She doesn't even look at Bhatti, doesn't say a word, and Alex can't stand it any longer.

"We're leaving," he says, heading to the door, hoping Maya will follow. Hoping she won't hate him for being right.

She takes Bhatti's limp hand, holds it for a brief moment. "You're going to wake up," she tells him. "You're going to be so proud." Her voice wavers, not enough to hear. Only enough to feel.

The guard watches as they pass. Maya keeps her eyes ahead.

They're halfway down the block when the message comes through: Protocol contained. For now.

For now.

Maya stares at Alex, and there's no I told you so in her eyes. No anything, just disbelief.

"You ever going to trust me?" she asks, her voice flat and raw and nothing like it was last night.

"No," he says.

This time, he means it.

CHAPTER THIRTEEN: LOOSE ENDS

GHOSTLY WHITE AND DISINFECTED, the room seems to stretch, to yawn, as if to swallow them all. DS Bhatti looks small against the crisp sheets, a shrunken man crumpled beneath plastic tubes and sterile bandages. His words, strained and trembling, emerge in fits and starts as he tells Maya and Alex that he's retiring from active service.

"Good to see you," he breathes, nodding to Maya, then Alex. The effort etches fresh lines into his face. "Expected you sooner."

"Had to lose a tail," Maya says, voice light but edged. She sets a bunch of flowers on the table, awkward among the beeping machines.

Bhatti tries a smile, more grimace than grin. "Never doubted you."

Maya glances at Alex. He's stationed near the door, scanning the hallway.

She moves closer to the bed, eyes on Bhatti. "How are you?"

Bhatti shifts against the pillows, a low hiss escaping as pain bites. "Intact," he says, eyes narrowing with irony. "For now."

The room hangs thick with antiseptic and unspoken questions. Bhatti watches them, chest rising and falling under the plastic tent of his gown. "Can't fight like this," he says. "I'm done."

"Don't say that." Maya's voice catches, then steadies. "You just need time."

"Not this time." Bhatti's eyes lock onto hers, fierce despite his frailty. "It's over."

Maya stands stiff, not knowing what to say. Bhatti's head dips, then rises, a nod made slow and deliberate by effort.

"Listen," he says, leaning back, gathering himself. "My last case. Yours now."

He reaches under the sheet, hand trembling, retrieves a flash drive. "Here," he says, extending it toward Maya. His arm shakes with the effort, and the drive dangles like an accusation. "Take it."

Maya hesitates, as if taking it seals Bhatti's fate. Then she steps forward, grips the drive. Her hand brushes his. It's warm but trembling.

"The Silent Protocol," Bhatti says, the words like pebbles ground from his throat. "Names. Proof. Enough to bury them all."

Maya's grip tightens around the drive. She holds it like a lifeline, like a promise. "This is—"

"Explosive," Bhatti cuts in. His breath rattles. "Use it wisely. They'll come after you."

Alex glances back, face taut. "Same ones who put you here?"

Bhatti's eyes flick to Alex. His answer is a look, sharp and loaded. Then back to Maya, each word weighted. "Be ready."

"We will be." Maya's voice is hard now, all fear squeezed out. "You know we will."

The machines hum their steady chorus. The tension makes the air brittle.

"Watch Gage," Bhatti says, his last words fierce and soft. "He's more than he seems."

The words linger. Maya nods, unsure what they mean but sure of their importance. She squeezes the drive until it leaves a mark in her palm. Bhatti closes his eyes, exhaustion draping him like a shroud.

Alex stands by the door, eyes darting from the hall back to Bhatti. "Maya," he says, a warning and a question.

She glances from Alex to Bhatti, back again. "I'm staying," she says, voice steady, almost defiant.

Bhatti's eyes flicker open, a dim light reignited. He studies her, the determination etched in her face, the way she plants herself by the bed like she belongs there, like she won't be moved.

"Stubborn," he murmurs, a shadow of a smile flitting across his lips. "Always were."

Maya sits, tension easing in her shoulders but not in her eyes. "Comes from the best," she says, returning the ghost of a smile.

Bhatti's breath catches, a brief tremor that stills almost as soon as it starts. He watches her with a strange mix of pride and worry.

"There's more," he says, voice a whisper now, brittle but insistent. "Dig deeper. Don't trust anyone."

She nods, and Bhatti's eyes close again, the struggle pulling him under. He is pale against the sheets, colourless, a figure bleached into the sterile background. But his presence looms large, even as it dwindles, an absence growing to fill the space he leaves behind.

Alex steps forward, unwilling to leave but unwilling to stay. "They'll trace us," he says, every word cut clean and sharp. "He's right. We need to move."

Maya rises slowly, like breaking from a spell. She stands by the bed a moment longer, just looking, as if to memorise Bhatti's lines, the crags of his features, the sharpness of his gaze, the steadiness it has given her. She lets go of the drive long enough to tuck the flowers into the sterile bedside cup.

"We'll be back," she promises. Bhatti stirs, a slight, involuntary twitch, too weak to be a nod, too strong to be nothing at all.

Alex opens the door, peers into the hallway. It's as white and endless as the room, gaping and echoing. A place where whispers can't live, where footsteps vanish into thick air.

Maya follows him out, her last glance a thread, tenuous and pulled taut between Bhatti's tired, determined eyes and the future they must make on their own. The sound of distant sirens follows them down the antiseptic corridor, a reminder, a threat, a promise.

THE ROOM SHRINKS AROUND her, closing in with shadows and clutter. Coffee cups jostle for space with takeout containers and overflowing ashtrays. Maya hunches over her laptop, the glow catching her face and setting it ablaze with determination as she pieces together Bhatti's information.

The keys clack like gunshots in the close space. Each stroke of the keyboard, a step closer to detonation. She scrolls through folders, pulls up images and documents. Cross-references with sources, matches names to scandals, emails to dates. Her fingers blur, speed fuelled by urgency and too much caffeine.

"The network maps," she mutters, mostly to herself. "They line up with—"

"Page six," Alex cuts in, not looking up from the window. "You covered it."

"Not enough," Maya says. "Not nearly."

Alex paces, footsteps light but constant, an orbit of protection and restlessness. "You should slow down."

"Can't."

Her desk is a battlefield of clutter. Takeout containers bleed sauce onto printouts. Half-empty cups of cold coffee compete for space. A tangle of cables, wires, conspiracy. The hum of the laptop the only steady thing. She glares at the screen, at the damning connections she drags to light.

"Listen to this," she says. Her eyes are dark smudges against her skin. Her focus a knife's edge. "Minister from 2017 memo? Tied to offshore account."

Alex finally turns. "That's big."

"Everything's big." She pauses, lets out a breath like she's been holding it for days. "Gage. Knew he'd come up."

"But can you prove it?"

"We can." She lifts a page, covered in scrawled notes, holds it like a torch in a cave. "We will."

Her words fill the small space, pushing against the walls, against the doubt, the fear. The room is dense with the urgency of their work. The laptop blinks an alert, a digital alarm urging her on. She squints, scrutinises. Each new lead a fresh nail in the coffin.

"They'll expect a leak," Alex says, a steady, unyielding calm in his voice. "Not this."

"That's the point." She types faster, faster, as if speed alone could save them.

The cursor moves with dizzying speed. Links embedded, paragraphs tweaked and reshaped. Headline a punch to the throat:

Silent Protocol Exposed: Politicians' Secret Surveillance Operation.

"They'll hit back," Alex warns.

"Let them," Maya fires back. She has not slept. Has not thought about sleeping.

The work spreads before her, a map of lies and greed and power. She follows each trail, backtracks, finds new routes, cuts and splices, makes the picture whole. Her movements are swift and sharp, as if guided by something more than determination. An obsession. A need.

The final words drop into place. She scans it one last time, a missile readied for launch. Her hand hovers over the keyboard, a moment suspended in time.

"Do it," Alex says, closer now.

And she does. Hits "publish." A single stroke, all the power of a bomb.

Her phone explodes with notifications. Social media alight with reactions, retweets, shares. She can barely keep up, the screen scrolling itself into a blur. Major news sites flash the headline, the story surging through the digital bloodstream.

"It's everywhere," she says, a stunned kind of triumph in her voice.

Alex nods, his vigilance briefly eclipsed by a glimmer of relief. "You did it."

"We did it," she insists, her exhaustion momentarily lifting, replaced by something bright, fierce, fragile.

They look at each other, a moment of shared victory stretching out, filling the cramped room with its tension and release. Then Maya leans back, letting out a breath, a long, ragged sigh that carries days of worry and fear with it.

"It's done," she says, almost a whisper, the words alien in her mouth.

She closes the laptop, the glow fading, leaving the room dimmer, smaller. The mess more vivid now without the digital light.

"Now we wait," Alex says, settling beside her, watchful but not tense, not yet.

Maya picks up her phone, reads the flood of responses, feels the weight of what they've done settle in. But so does the uncertainty, the knowledge that they have no idea what will follow.

"It's going viral," she says, disbelief mingling with hope. "I can't believe—"

"You better," Alex cuts in. "Soon as they do."

Maya shakes her head, still in shock. "Maybe—"

"Don't," Alex interrupts, his voice as tight and careful as his gaze. "Don't start hoping. Not yet."

"What's that supposed to mean?"

He looks at her, steady, unflinching. "You know what it means."

"Yeah," Maya admits. Her excitement ebbs a little, replaced by the reality, the waiting. But not all of it. Not yet. She tosses her phone aside. "But until they do—"

She lets the words trail off, unfinished, a challenge thrown into the dark. They sit in silence, anticipation gnawing at the edges. Around them, the clutter of their struggle piles high, testament to the days and nights and fears they've put into this. It's over. It's not.

"We'll sleep when we're dead," Alex finally says, a hint of a wry smile breaking the tension.

Maya leans back, a small smile ghosting her lips, the fight already igniting in her eyes again. "Promises, promises."

ONE HOUR LATER

The room feels emptier, darker, as if something vital has been siphoned out. Maya slouches over her laptop, hitting refresh like it could bring the world back to life. But the article is gone, vanished from every platform, every site, every screen.

"It can't be," she whispers, voice thin and stretched.

Alex is by the window, watching the night through eyes that grow harder by the second. "It's gone?"

"Not possible." She hits refresh again. Again. Desperation driving the motion, a perpetual cycle of disbelief. "They can't just—"

"Did." Alex says.

Her phone is a dead weight in her hand. Notifications stalled. The viral surge smothered, extinguished. It's like watching something come alive and die in the same breath.

"Every site," she says, the words hollowed out and raw. "It's like it never—"

"Existed," Alex finishes, bitter. He's moving now, quick and agitated, but his eyes never leave her, the room, the threat.

Maya's fingers are pale spiders crawling over keys. She types furiously, biting her lip until she tastes blood. "I'll fix it," she says, voice shaky, desperate. "I'll put it back."

"They're too fast," Alex snaps. "Too strong."

"Then we fight back!" She dials a number, hears only silence. Her frustration spikes, a sharp, brittle thing. She throws the phone onto the table; watches it land among the detritus of their short-lived triumph. "No one answers," she says, disbelief turning her voice thin and sharp. "They're all—"

"Gone," Alex says, every word cut clean and sharp. "Just like that."

"Don't," she warns, even as she knows it's true. She pushes her chair back, scrambles for cables, hard drives, anything with a whisper of hope. "We'll find it," she insists, less sure, more frantic.

"Can you hear yourself?" Alex demands, his voice a storm barely contained. "They killed it, Maya. We can't—"

"Watch me," she spits back, anger giving her momentum.

But everywhere she looks, there's nothing. No article. No trace. She dives into backup servers, digital depths that promise more silence. They crash, blink out of existence like lights snapped off one by one.

"How?" she chokes, clutching the edge of the desk, white-knuckled. "Who—?"

"Someone with power," Alex says. "Serious power." He's next to her now, a tether she can't feel but can't let go of. "Think."

Maya's head drops to her hands, breath shaky and uneven. "It's not possible," she repeats, as if saying it could make it true, as if refusing to accept it could keep it from being real.

Alex grips her shoulder, the contact startling and grounding. "It's what Bhatti warned us about," he says, gentler but no less urgent. "You knew this was coming."

Maya's eyes lift, meet his with a wild, desperate defiance. "Not like this," she says, almost a whisper, the fight dimming.

Her phone pings once. Twice. The sound cuts through the room, through their disbelief, stops them cold. Alex and Maya lock eyes, the same wary understanding flickering, then igniting. They both reach for it, for the sound, the connection, the possibility. But the message finds them first.

The true enemy isn't Gage. It's who built him.

The text burns bright against the dim, a flare that blinds and disorients. Then gone, a ghost, a mirage, a taunt.

Maya stares at her screen, at the void where the words had been. Her hands tremble, the vibration spreading, consuming. "What does it—?"

"You know," Alex cuts in, jaw set, words flat and cold. "You know exactly what it means."

The silence thickens around them, the room a vacuum of certainty and sound. Maya shudders, the reality sinking deeper, roots taking hold in her chest. "I don't," she says, a last gasp of hope, the word small, shrinking.

"You do." Alex's voice doesn't flinch, but something else in him does. Something quiet. Something not quite fear. "Whoever sent this—"

"They know," Maya finishes, the truth finally settling in. Her eyes darken, narrow, refocus. "They know every-thing."

The fight returns, creeping, then surging. The implica-tions unravel, knot, fray. She tries to piece them together, but they spin too fast. Her breathing steadies, the ragged edges smoothing out into resolve.

Alex leans closer, every muscle in him ready to bolt, or strike, or run. "They're telling us," he says, trying to keep up with the sharp turns, the quick change in direction, "Gage isn't our only—"

"Enemy," Maya says. The word fits now. Heavy, sure. Real. "He's just a pawn."

Alex straightens, as if this realisation had hit him, and hit him hard. "Bigger than we thought," he admits, the anger gone, replaced by a grim acceptance.

"Always is." Maya's voice is steadier now, though noth-ing else is. "We push them, they push back."

"We push harder," Alex says, but the room feels emptier still, as if the space itself doubts him.

Maya opens the laptop again, looks at the blankness of the screen, feels the blankness trying to claim her. Her fingers pause, hesitate, then dive in again.

Alex grabs his coat, eyes the window, the hallway, everything with suspicion. "They know where we are," he says. "If they know this much, they—"

Another ping, but this one not a message. Farther away. Police or something worse.

"You think they—?"

"Don't wait to find out," Alex snaps, already in motion.

But Maya's at the laptop, like there's still time, like there's still hope. The lights blink as if mocking her. She stays at the keys. Her mind burns through the layers, the networks, the traps. "You go," she says, but not like she means it.

"Maya!" Alex shouts, but the word has no power over her.

The sound of sirens, urgent and angry, bleeds through the thin walls. It's too much like the silence. It's too much like everything they thought they'd escaped.

"One minute," she insists, and the determination he hates, loves, fears, pulls him back to her side.

"Thirty seconds," Alex concedes, his urgency fighting hers.

The world shrinks around them, dangerous and real, and this time, Maya hits the keys like she's fighting not to lose it but to stay alive.

The End

Preview of Book Three in the Trilogy

Chapter One: Whispers in the Dark

Rain peppers the windows in sporadic bursts. Maya leans closer to the screen, scouring the lines of text for a connection that isn't there. The words blur from exhaustion and resolve. Notes pile up, relentless and unorganised, but her instincts are too honed to let her mind slip. Someone, somewhere, is going down for this. The vibration of a phone on silent rips through her concentration.

A haphazard mountain of paper and empty cups surrounds her. Maya doesn't notice. She's too absorbed in the screen, trying to unpick layers of lies and deception. Hours stretch. Details sharpen and soften, depending on caffeine levels and adrenaline. She runs a finger along the latest set of printouts, lips moving as she processes the latest find. It's all there... just disconnected. Somewhere in this mess, there's a story that will tear apart a billion-dollar empire. But right now, it's a blurry headache.

Another vibration from the phone. A notification, not a call. This time, it makes her look up. Outside, a bike courier speeds off, tyres hissing on wet pavement. He's left something at the door.

Maya's up and moving, suspicion and curiosity in her every step. She stands over the package, no return address, nothing but her name scrawled across it. The ink smudges slightly as she picks it up. There's weight to it. Uncertain. Anticipation mixes with paranoia as she locks the door behind her.

Back at the desk, the laptop casts her face in cold blue light. The package opens with a rip of tearing paper. A thumb drive clatters onto her keyboard. She doesn't breathe. Her first instinct is to scan it. Her second is to panic. Anything could be on this drive. Anything and nothing. It's bait, a trap, or the key to breaking everything wide open.

She digs into her drawer, pulls out a small device, and plugs the drive into it first. Fingers drum impatient rhythms on the desk as it checks for malware. Seconds pass like hours. The green light blinks on, and she allows herself the ghost of a smile. Not this time. She isn't getting burned.

One click, and she's pulled back into her world. The file name is in all caps: "THE FINAL CIPHER." Cryptic, no pun intended. She sits back and lets the chair support her weight for the first time in hours. Exhaustion begs her to look away, to sleep, but she's running on nerves now.

Opening the file brings up a wall of code and encrypted data. It's nothing she's seen before—structured, intricate, impenetrable. Maya's mind races. There's something familiar about this. A puzzle she knows she can't solve alone.

Her thoughts drift, piecing together years of memories, of leads gone cold and questions unanswered. GageCorp. It always leads back there. She leans forward, a shadow crossing her face as the rain picks up outside. The glow of the screen reflects in her eyes, and they flash with something that could be fear, could be excitement.

Maya doesn't waste time. If she's right, this changes everything. She ejects the thumb drive with the care of a surgeon. It disappears into a hidden compartment of her desk, nested in with a web of notes and backup files. More layers. More security.

Her chair scrapes loudly against the floor as she rises, but she doesn't care. She's already reaching for a phone, one of several identical models scattered across the table. No traceable lines. She isn't taking chances. Her hands tremble with the pent-up energy of revelation. She's one step closer, and the stakes have never been higher.

When the number's punched in, she hesitates. It's been too long. The message tone is familiar, brisk, encoded. She doesn't bother with niceties.

"Got something. Meet?"

She sends it and drops the phone back on the desk. No need to watch it for a reply. She knows he'll come through. A pause, then the message rings out:

Usual place. 48 hours.

Time to breathe. Time to dig deeper. Maya stares at the screen, but her mind is on the thumb drive. On the way it connects everything. On the way it threatens everything.

Someone, somewhere, is going down for this.

THE WAREHOUSE GROANS WITH each gust of wind, straining against its own decay. Alex waits in the dark, breath visible in the damp air. It takes her a second to see him, and another for him to step forward. They pause, staring at each other like ghosts.

Rain taps at the metal roof like impatient fingers. His figure sharpens in the shadow. Thinner, she thinks, and quicker to disappear. Alex steps closer, hands stuffed in the pockets of a rain-soaked jacket, every movement controlled and deliberate. His beard's new, but the look in his eyes isn't.

"Maya," he says. A simple statement, almost a question.

She shifts the bag on her shoulder, wary. "You look like shit."

"So do you." He allows himself a grin but then relaxes the facial muscles as he remembers their history. Too much baggage weighing it down.

Maya takes him in. The same measured intensity, the same ready posture, like he's always waiting for something to go wrong. "I didn't think you'd show."

He shrugs. "Didn't think you'd ask."

Silence settles in, wraps around them, almost as tangible as the rain. Her eyes never leave his. Tension vibrates through the air, unbroken, as they stand there, worlds apart and inches away. She finally reaches into her bag, pulling out the drive. It dangles from her fingers for a moment, and she feels his hesitation.

"What are you waiting for?" Her voice cracks the silence like a whip.

Their fingers touch, barely, as he takes it from her. It's a shock, but he hides it well. Not like before.

Alex doesn't waste time. A small metal case appears from under his coat, and he slots the drive into a custom port. The glow of the screen colours his face a pale blue, washing out his features until he almost looks unfamiliar.

"Where did you get this?" he asks sharply, eyes never leaving the scrolling data.

"Package at the door," Maya replies. "No return address."

"Too easy." His fingers work at the device, pulling up more screens, diving deeper.

She steps closer, watching him work. "Could say the same about you."

Alex gives her a sidelong glance, half amused, half something else. "Trust issues?"

"You taught me well."

He nods, almost approvingly, then turns back to the drive. "These encryption patterns..."

He doesn't finish. A moment hangs in the air between them, heavy and expectant.

"What about them?"

He holds her gaze, and for a second, she's sure he's going to lie. But when he finally speaks, the truth cuts through the room like a blade.

"They're Nightfall signatures."

The words hit like a fist, and Maya takes an involuntary step back. "Nightfall," she repeats, processing the implication. Her mind races, recalling everything she's dug up about the secretive MI5 programme, everything she couldn't prove.

"They told you it was shut down," she says, her voice a mix of accusation and disbelief.

"Years ago," Alex replies, running a hand through damp hair. "Someone's using Nightfall protocols. Recent ones."

His proximity pulls her back, his body a warm, solid presence in the cold room. She looks at the screen again, but her thoughts are on him. His connection to all this. Their connection. Everything as tangled and encrypted as the data they're staring at.

"Got a theory?" Alex asks, trying to sound casual. Failing.

"A few," Maya says, and her lip curls into the kind of smile that's only skin deep. "You hear the rumours?"

He shakes his head, still focused on the data. "Been out of the loop."

Maya inches closer, her breath catching slightly. "They say Gage is alive."

The reaction is subtle. A tightening of his jaw. A narrowing of his eyes. She doesn't need more.

"Sources claim he's recruiting offshore," she continues. "Tech dissidents. Rogue operatives."

Alex turns to her, the space between them impossibly charged. "If he has access to Nightfall..." He trails off again, but Maya fills in the blanks.

They're too close now, examining the code and each other. He moves to take a step back, then doesn't.

"Is this about him?" Maya's voice is lower, urgent. "Is that why you've gone dark?"

Alex shakes his head, though the motion is uncertain. "If he's alive, it changes everything."

She lets the words hang there, knowing the weight of them. "We need to decode this," she insists. Her hand reaches for his shoulder, and the moment stretches until it almost snaps.

"I'll need specialised equipment," Alex says. "More time."

"48 hours?"

He nods. The energy between them is too raw, too volatile. He needs to look away but doesn't.

"You going to disappear again?"

"Will you trust me if I don't?"

Maya's silence is its own answer. She holds his gaze until it's too much, then turns for the door.

Alex watches her go, tension unwinding with each of her steps. He knows this is a bad idea, knows the risks. But she asked, and he answered. He can't help himself.

The rain sounds different once she's gone.

The Final Cipher releases on June 26, 2025, and is the final instalment of *The Last Message Trilogy*. It can be pre-ordered at all major online retailers here at Books2Read.

STEPHEN
BENTLEY

THE
FINAL
CIPHER

A Request

I sincerely hope you enjoyed reading this book as much as I enjoyed writing it. If you did, I would greatly appreciate a short review on the sales platform where you bought it Reviews are crucial for any author, and even just a line or two can make a huge difference.

If you would like to receive Stephen's newsletter, click here.Alternatively, please use the QR code below.

Mailing List

About Stephen Bentley

Stephen Bentley is an award-winning author. Of his first true crime novel, UNDERCOVER, screenwriter and novelist, writer of 'Julie' BBC Drama, Rob Gittins, said, "The fascinating and extraordinary inside story from the man who was actually there."

Of his later fiction works, British crime author, Pat MacDonald said, "I knew when I read the author's first book 'Undercover: Operation Julie' although non-fiction that he could make the transition to writing fiction; I was right. He has an ease of language that lends itself to storytelling; he tells it as if he was there in the plot and why shouldn't he having been an undercover cop in the real world? Not that Steve Regan is meant to be him, but having the experience means he can do whatever he wants with his fictional characters, and they will always be believable."

Like some other authors, his life experience is broad and unconventional. He spent 30 years in the legal system, first as a detective for 15 years then as barrister plying his trade as "a wig for hire" in London and the English provinces.

He was a pioneering undercover cop on Operation Julie and as a barrister defended in trials involving murder, rape, drug importation, other serious crimes and defended soldiers at courts-martial.

He worked in a warehouse. Rode a big motorbike as a London courier. He drove big articulated trucks and taught how to drive them. He also worked as a hospital porter twice. He drove chilled delivery vans in London in the 1990s to fund his law degree and bar school studies. He spent the last two years of his working life driving plant and operating heavy filtration machinery for Europe's largest water company. His work mates soon recognised his advocacy skills and elected him as their shop steward.

He has now written over twenty books. Two of them have been optioned and in development; one as a TV drama series, and one as a drama doc.

His wife is a better person than him in all regards and is a source of support in his goal of entertaining readers. She has also made him a better person.

For new releases and news about the Operation Julie TV series/documentary, you may wish to subscribe to Stephen's newsletter here. Or use the QR code below:

STEPHEN BENTLEY MAILING LIST

Stephen now has a Ko-Fi page where members have exclusive access to (1) serialisation of all his future releases before publication in all his pen names, (2) a free digital copy of those releases, and (3) exclusive discounts on merch and bespoke products. Use that link or the QR code below to access the page.

Stephen's Ko-Fi Page

Now a multi-genre author, Stephen also writes cozy mysteries in the pen name of KJ Cornwall.

You can listen to Stephen talking about his Operation Julie undercover days on the BBC Radio 4 Life Changing programme/podcast available 24/7 worldwide on BBC Sounds. And on the same platform, he also contributes to Acid Dream: The Great LSD Plot.

Also by Stephen Bentley

You can find all of Stephen Bentley's books here on his website where his catalogue is kept updated.
They include his bestselling true crime books and crime fiction series including:
The Steve Regan Undercover Cop Thrillers
The Detective Matt Deal Thrillers
L.A. Cyber Noir Mysteries
The Last Message Trilogy
You may also find his books here at Booklinker including those written in a pen name. Alternatively, use the QR code below to access the same page.